As Ever,
BOOKY

Bernice Thurman Hunter

Cover photo by Gordon Wyatt

Scholastic-TAB Publications Ltd.
123 Newkirk Road, Richmond Hill, Ontario
Canada

Canadian Cataloguing in Publication Data

Hunter, Bernice Thurman
    As ever, Booky

ISBN 0-590-71547-X

I. Title

PS8565.U57A77 1985   jC813'.54   C85-098480-7
PZ7.H86As 1985

1st printing 1985   **Printed in Canada**

Contents

To Lloyd, with love

1
Guess what!

"Guess what, Mum?"

"What, Bea?" Mum always looked startled when I began a conversation that way.

"Nothing to worry about, Mum — just the opposite. Remember me telling you I made a new friend on the first day of school?" I was in second form at Runnymede Collegiate.

"Yes. Gloria Somebody-or-other," Mum recalled as she expertly pinched the edge of a piecrust.

"Gloria Carlyle. Isn't that a glorious name? It sounds like a screen star's name, doesn't it? Like Carole Lombard or Jean Harlow. I wish I had a romantic name like that. Anyway, Gloria's father owns a whole chain of hardware stores and her mother has a housemaid and plays tennis every day. And guess who lives right next door to them?"

"For mercy sakes, how should I know? I can't stand around playing guessing games when it's nigh on suppertime." Nudging me aside with her round hip, she opened the oven door and turned the gas on full blast. Then she struck a wooden match on the sandpaper strip along the side of the Eddy box and poked the flame into the hole in the oven floor. It lit with a bang. But she turned it down too quickly and it went out. "Drat!" she declared and repeated the whole process.

Closing the oven door, she turned her attention back to me. Her face was red from scurrying. Damp, dark curls, threaded with grey, clung to her high forehead. "Well, Bea, are you ever going to tell me who lives next door to glorious Gloria?"

"Aw, Mum, don't make fun of her. She's really nice for a rich person." I let a few seconds drift dramatically by, but then I saw that Mum was getting irritated, so I exclaimed rapturously, "L.M. Montgomery!"

"No!" Her stunned reaction was all I could have hoped for. "Not the woman who wrote *Anne of Green Gables?*"

"Yes! But that's not all!"

"What do you mean, not all?" Her dark eyes were flashing with interest now.

"Well, Gloria told Mrs. Macdonald about me — that's her married name. Her real name is Lucy Maud Montgomery, but her husband is the Reverend Ewan Macdonald. And she's got children too, Mum. Imagine having L.M. Montgomery for a mother!" I saw a hurt look flit across her flushed face, so I added quickly, "But I still think you're the most perfect mother in the world, Mum."

"Oh, pshaw, Booky" — that's what Mum used to call me when I was a kid, *Boo*-key and every now and then it still slipped out — "I'm a far cry from perfect. But it's nice you think so." She reached up (I was

2

taller than she was) and pinched my cheek with floury fingers. "Are you ever going to tell me what this is all about?"

"Oh, sorry, Mum. Well, Gloria told L.M. — I mean Mrs. Macdonald — all about me. You know, how I'm always writing stories and that she's my favourite author — stuff like that. And do you know what she said?"

"Bea, stop asking me questions I can't answer and lend me a hand here. Either that or get out of my road." She bustled past me to the kitchen cabinet, pulled the flour bin out on its hinges and scooped up another cupful of flour.

So I blurted out the rest. "She said Gloria could bring me over to her house for tea!"

"Sakes alive!" Mum whirled around, rubbing her hands together in that excited way she had, sending mists of flour floating through the air. "When?"

"Saturday afternoon. *This* Saturday afternoon."

"Oh, my stars, what will you wear?" Mum popped the pie into the oven. "You'll just have to get busy and let down your navy skirt. You'll need to look your best to meet such a grand lady." Her voice was positively reverent. She had almost a holy respect for people of letters, and she liked L.M. Montgomery's books nearly as much as I did. "If you get the chance," she added diffidently, "tell her your mother greatly admires Judy Plum in *Pat of Silver Bush*."

"Tell who?" My brother Arthur came in just in time to catch the tail end of the conversation.

"Bea's been invited to meet L.M. Montgomery!" Mum announced proudly. The way she said it you'd think I'd been invited to Buckingham Palace.

"Who's that?" asked Arthur, piling his school books on a kitchen chair. He was in fourth form and he had tons of homework.

"Oh, good grief, don't show your ignorance." I gave Arthur a disgusted look. "She's just the most famous author in Canada, that's all."

"You're nuts!" he scoffed. "Ralph Connor is."

"He is not!"

"He is so!"

"Who is so?" Nine-year-old Jakey had come high-tailing it up from the cellar to see what all the fuss was about.

"Oh, you're too young to understand, Jakey." I brushed him aside impatiently.

"I am not!" he cried, his dark eyes blazing.

"You are so!" Five-year-old Billy's squeaky voice came up from under the table where he was playing cars.

"Stop it, all of you!" Mum yelled, scattering cutlery onto the oilcloth-covered table. "Arthur, get at your homework. Bea, finish laying this table. Jakey and Billy, scoot down to the cellar out of my sight before I skin you alive. Your father and sister will be home any minute and I haven't even got the stew thickened yet, let alone the dumplings made."

Dad had been working steady as a maintenance man at Neilson's Chocolate Factory for over three years now. At the beginning of the new year, 1937, he had had his wages raised from fourteen to sixteen dollars a week because he was such a good worker. After weathering all those grim Depression years, a steady job with good pay was something my parents didn't take for granted. Dad said he hoped he'd never have to stand in a food line again as long as he lived.

When we were on the pogey he had to walk all the way downtown with our food voucher. Then he had to carry a potato sack full of tinned goods over his shoulder all the way home again. It was ten miles from our house to the food station, but the pogey didn't allow for streetcar tickets.

My sister Willa had a job now too. She had finished fifth form with top honours. Then, when she knew there was no hope of affording university, she went back to high school and took the three-year commercial course in one year. Now she was a receptionist in a doctor's office — as close as she would ever come to her dream of being a doctor. She earned twelve dollars a week, with Saturday afternoons off. Every Saturday night, like clockwork, she handed Mum six dollars board money. Mum was tickled pink.

The first time Willa paid her, she looked around the spotless kitchen, her eyes bright with longing. "Maybe someday we'll have enough money to buy this place from Billy Sundy," she said. Billy Sundy was our landlord.

"We'd need two hundred dollars to put down," Dad said hopelessly. "It might just as well be two thousand." There went Mum's fondest dream up in smoke again.

"I'll buy it for you when I get big, Mum," Billy promised solemnly.

"That's nice, Billy-bo-bingo," she'd said, squeezing his cheeks so his lips opened up like a fish's.

The second my sister set foot in the door I said, "Who's the most famous Canadian author, Willa?"

Without hesitation she answered, "L.M. Montgomery."

"See, Arthur!" I hooted triumphantly. He let out

a loud moan and banged his head on the dining room table where he was doing his homework.

I told Willa my news and she was really impressed, which made up for Arthur's stupidity. Even Dad, who didn't know much about books and authors, had heard about L.M. Montgomery, so he gave me some advice. "Now, Bea, you're inclined to be a chatterbox" — I groaned inwardly but didn't interrupt — "so try to hold your tong." That was his old-fashioned way of saying tongue, and no amount of criticism would make him change it. "If you listen to the lady, she might be able to help you with your writing. And be sure to ask for her autograph. It might be worth something someday."

It was only Monday. I thought the week would never end.

2
Tea and advice

At exactly one o'clock on Saturday I met Gloria on the corner of Jane and Bloor. She looked gorgeous in her new tunic with the razor-sharp pleats and her red velvet jacket. Her stylish outfit made me acutely aware of my old navy pleatless skirt and blue sweater, neatly darned at the elbows. But Mum had painstakingly turned the collar and cuffs of my white blouse, so it looked almost as good as new.

The night before I had done up my fine hair in pin curls and it had combed out kind of frizzy, but not too bad. I had wet my eyelashes with vaseline, which made them look thicker and longer, and put on two layers of lip rouge. (Willa said not to use too much or I might look cheap.) I couldn't do a thing about the shape of my nose, but on the whole I was quite pleased with myself.

Under my arm I carried a grammar-school workbook with my latest story penned carefully inside. The title was "Victoria, the Girl Who Never Told a Lie in Her Life." I was sure it was the best thing I'd ever written.

Veering left off Bloor Street we walked along a tree-lined avenue, called Riverside Drive, on the banks of the Humber. It was a beautiful, winding road with rolling lawns and weeping willows, and no sidewalks. The houses were big and far apart. Glittering stone driveways curved up to wide, two-car garages.

On Veeny Street in Swansea, the little village on the western outskirts of Toronto where I lived, we didn't have garages. Our houses were so tightly packed together there was barely enough room for alleyways between. But it didn't matter because nobody on Veeny Street owned a car anyway.

Gloria stopped in front of a magnificent mansion where a man was busy raking up a pile of red and gold leaves. "That's my house," she said, a bit smugly I thought.

"Is that your father?" I asked innocently.

"No! That's Willy, the gardener."

Willy the gardener tipped his cap to Gloria, then stared me up and down as if I was an oddity on Riverside Drive.

Gloria pointed to the house next door. "That's where the Macdonalds live," she said matter-of-factly.

I gazed, speechless, at a white stone house with gabled windows, all hemmed in by shrubs and trees and flowers. A rustic sign nailed to a fence post read *Journey's End*.

At that moment the dark wooden door swung open and out stepped a regal lady who looked for all the world like Queen Mary, the king's mother, even to the long string of pearls looped twice around her neck. She smiled and beckoned to us and my heart did somersaults.

"She looks like a genius!" I whispered.

"She is!" my friend agreed knowingly.

Gloria introduced us. "Mrs Macdonald, this is my friend Bee-triss." (She had wonderful manners, but terrible pronunciation. The way she said my name made it sound like a vegetable!)

"I'm pleased to meet you, Beatrice." It sounded entirely different coming from *her*. She reached out and took my hand, and my legs turned to jelly.

Completely forgetting Dad's well-meant advice, I started to babble. "Oh, Miss Montgomery, I love all your books and I've read every one at least twice, some of them three times, and I especially love *Emily Climbs* and *Anne of Avonlea*. My mother loves *Pat of Silver Bush* best and she told me to tell you if I got the chance that she greatly admires Judy Plum. But I personally adore *The Story Girl* and *Kilmeny of the Orchard* and *The Blue Castle* — oh, Barney was so romantic — and I hope you have time to write a hundred more books because I think you're the greatest writer the world has ever known."

Luckily, I ran out of breath.

"That's very kind of you, Beatrice, and do thank your mother for her compliment about Judy Plum." She spoke just as if I'd said something perfectly sensible. "Gloria tells me that you're a story girl too. Come into the garden and we'll talk about it."

We followed her down a white gravel path that led to a backyard filled with daisies and chrysanthemums and evergreens. At the foot of one big pine tree was a smooth granite rock with the word *Lucky* painted on it.

"That stone was shipped up to me from my home in Prince Edward Island," the author explained softly, "and under it my dear little pussycat lies sleeping. He was my inseparable companion for fourteen years and I miss him sorely."

Suddenly I was consumed with jealousy over the bones of that old dead cat.

As we sat down on red cedar chairs, I felt a splinter snag my silk stocking — or I should say Willa's. I had no silk stockings, just lisle, and I had borrowed Willa's best pair. Only she didn't know it yet.

I was trying desperately to think of something intelligent to say when the back door was pushed open by a woman's behind. Out she came with a loaded tray and set the table with china dishes, silver spoons and a fancy teapot with little legs on it. Then she set two glass plates within easy reach. One held sandwiches and the other teacakes.

"Thank you, Marny," Mrs. Macdonald said, then to me, "Cream and sugar, Beatrice?"

"Yes, please." We never had real cream at home, just milk.

She put the cream and sugar in the cup first, then poured the tea. Mum never did that.

"Help yourselves, girls," she said. Then she leaned back, casually sipping her tea as if she had nothing better to do than entertain two schoolgirls, when all the time I knew there was another great novel churning around in her head just dying to get out.

I watched Gloria surreptitiously and copied everything she did. She spread a linen napkin on her lap, so I did too. She took two sandwiches, so I did too — a three-cornered egg-salad with the crusts cut off and a green-cheese pinwheel. Green cheese! Imagine!

I had never tasted anything so delectable. We ate six sandwiches. When Mrs. Macdonald offered us more Gloria politely refused. So I did too, even though I could easily have eaten the whole works in two minutes flat. Then we each had another cup of tea and a teacake. The pink icing cracked when you bit into it. Inside, it was soft and white as a marshmallow.

Finally Marney came and cleared it all away.

"May I see your work, Beatrice?" asked Mrs. Macdonald suddenly. My work? At first I didn't know what she meant. Then I followed her eyes to my notebook. My hand shook as I passed it to her.

The pages rustled as she turned them. Sunlight filtered through the leaves and glinted on her silver hair. Gloria and I slanted glances at each other, but we didn't say a word. A bluebird flashed by almost close enough to touch.

Presently Mrs. Macdonald closed the book and removed her gold-rimmed glasses. "Your story is lovely, Beatrice." Her voice was gentle and kind, but I didn't like the word "lovely." I had hoped to hear "brilliant" or "witty" or just plain "excellent."

"My dear" — now her tone had become very serious — "allow me to give you some advice from my own experience. *Do* keep writing. You have a lively imagination and your characters ring true. But do not, I repeat, *do not* expect to publish at your tender age. The inevitable rejections would surely defeat you. Instead, channel your energies into your studies."

My heart sank. "But — but — it's more fun to write stories than do homework!" The stupid words were out before I could stop them.

"True. But your first priority must be your school work, because no one needs higher education more than a journalist. Will you remember that, Beatrice?"

"Yes, Miss Montgomery," I said, but I was already defeated. The thought of all that higher education struck terror in my heart. And besides, I was dying to be done with school so I could go out to work and make money to buy nice clothes like Gloria's.

We said goodbye, promising to come back soon. But I never did go back. And I'd even forgotten to get her autograph.

"Well, you dumb-bell, you wasted your whole Saturday afternoon," jeered Arthur. For once I agreed with him.

"Don't fret, Bea," Mum consoled me. "When you write Miss Montgomery your bread-and-butter note you can ask for her signature then."

So that's what I did. About three days later back came her reply in her own handwriting, which was so hard to read that I had to ask Willa to decipher it for me. In it she repeated her solemn advice and her compliment about my "lovely" story. The letter was signed *Sincerely, L.M. Montgomery Macdonald.*

I put it and my story far back on the closet shelf and didn't look at them again for years.

3
Mixed company

I went all melancholy for weeks after that. Then one day Mum snapped me out of it with a swell idea.

"How would you like a real grown-up party for your fifteenth birthday, Bea?" she asked.

"Really? Girls *and* boys?" I had never had an honest-to-goodness party before. Since Billy and I shared the same birthday, our celebrations were usually family affairs, with Aunt Milly or Aunt Maggie and their families for company.

"If Bea has a party, can I have one too?" begged Billy.

"Oh, I suppose so. But not on the same day. That would be too much of a good thing. You can have five friends for supper, Billy, since you'll be five years old. You're growing up at last, Billy-bo-bingo," she said, pinching his button nose shut so he had to wriggle it like a rabbit to get it unstuck. "I wouldn't trade you for all the tea in China, but I sure hope there's no more where you came from."

"Where did I come from, Mum?" Billy's blue Thomson eyes lit up with curiosity.

"Oh, oh, little pitchers have big ears!"

Mum was stymied by the unexpected question, so I jumped in and saved the day. "How many friends can I have, Mum, fifteen?"

"Mercy, no! This house is way too small for such a crowd. You'll have to make ten your limit, Bea."

Ten kids! It was more than I'd dared hope for.

That night I sat down at the dining room table and cut out neat squares of paper and began writing invitations in fancy script. Jakey was sitting across from me doing his homework.

Soon Billy came out from under the table and leaned his chin on my elbow curiously. "Whatcha doing, Bea-Bea?"

"Making invitations for my party, Bingo."

"Who's coming?"

"Oh, a bunch of my friends."

"Are you going to ask Roy-Roy the dumb-boy?"

"Billy, don't say Roy-Roy the dumb-boy. His name is Roy Butterbaugh."

Jakey looked up, glad of the interruption. "You call him that, Bea. Everybody does, because he don't know nothing."

"I used to call him that when I was young and silly," I admitted. "But you're wrong about him not knowing anything, Jakey. Roy-Roy knows more than he gets credit for."

Roy-Roy and his mother, Raggie Rachel (that's what all the kids called her because she wore four or five raggedy dresses piled on top of each other — she wasn't smelly or dirty, just raggedy), lived up Veeny Street in a tumbledown cottage that belonged to the village. They used to live in a shack down by Catfish

Pond and Rachel picked the dump for a living. Now she took in washing. Her backyard was always flapping with other people's bed sheets. She scrubbed by hand over a washboard, outside in summer, inside in winter. Mum said poor Rachel had a hard row to hoe.

No one seemed to know exactly what was wrong with Roy-Roy, only that he'd always been peculiar. His body jerked constantly and he slobbered and gabbled when he tried to talk. But I had found out years ago that if you listened really carefully he usually made perfect sense.

"Are you going to invite him?" Billy persisted.

"No, Billy, not this time."

"Why not? You always say he's your friend."

"Well, he is. But his mother wouldn't let him come anyway. She never lets him out of her sight anymore. And besides, he'd be embarrassed."

"Awww, he ain't smart enough to be embarrassed." Jakey was still unconvinced.

"Yes he is, Jakey. And if *you're* so darn smart, how come you keep saying dumb things like 'ain't' and 'don't know nothing'?"

Jakey stuck out his tongue and went back to his books, and Billy got bored and went away. So I finally got my invitations done.

Most of them were going to our gang on Veeny Street, but a few were addressed to new friends I'd made in high school. Gloria Carlyle was one, of course. And Lorne Huntley.

Lorne was the handsomest, most popular boy in Runnymede Collegiate (a "dreamboat," to quote Gloria), and to top it off, he was a football hero.

He had spoken to me only once, when he accidentally bumped into me on the staircase and knocked my books all over the place. He gathered them up and handed them back to me with a gorgeous grin and a "Sorry, kiddo!" Then he ran to catch up to his classmates. It was the nicest apology I'd ever had. But other than that we hadn't exchanged a word. So how I had the colossal gall to ask him to my party I'll never know.

Anyway, the next day I handed out the folded invitations between periods.

"What's this?" asked Lorne, flashing his incredible smile and running his long fingers carelessly through his curly brown hair.

"It's an invitation to my fifteenth birthday party." I faced him squarely so he wouldn't notice my bumpy nose, which all my life had been the bane of my existence. My heart beating like a triphammer, I added, "You don't have to come if you don't want to."

Darn! I was always saying dumb things like that.

"I'll be there with bells on," he promised. Then he went loping down the hall, leaving me gaping after him.

At first Gloria said she wasn't sure she could make it. Our friendship had cooled quite a bit since she realized that I would probably never be rich and famous like her neighbour. I was awfully disappointed in her, but Mum wasn't surprised. She said you couldn't mix oil and water. Anyway, when I told Gloria that Lorne was coming she quickly changed her mind and said she thought she could make it after all.

The Huntleys lived in a ritzy district known as Baby Point, where two big stone pillars stood like guardian angels at either side of the entranceway. So Gloria had decided that Lorne was her type.

Walking home from school that day with Gladie Cole, my cousin and best friend, I told her I had invited Lorne to my party.

"Geez, Bea," she marvelled, looking at me as if I'd just had an audience with the king, "I wouldn't have the nerve to ask him in a million years. Just seeing him in the halls makes me nervous as a cat."

"Well, maybe you'd better not come then," I teased.

"Wild horses wouldn't keep me away!" she hooted as we crossed Bloor Street and headed for Woolworth's, where a sign in the window read: *SPECIAL . . . Spanish peanuts, ten cents a pound!* Glad's mother had given her a nickel for a bottle of milk at lunchtime, so she bought half a pound.

"Are Ruth and Ada coming?"

"Sure." Ruth Vaughan, Ada-May Hubbard, Glad and I had been a foursome for years. Our houses were within a stone's throw of each other on dead-end Veeny Street, and we were all related in one way or another. But we had drifted apart since high school because Ruth and Ada were a year older than Glad and me, and they were in third form.

Even Arthur seemed interested in my party (that puzzled me a bit), and Willa helped Mum make about a hundred sandwiches. That's the kind of sister Willa was. We were five years apart, so we didn't have much in common, but she was always doing things for me. Mum said she took after no stranger. "She's like Mumma," she said, meaning her mother. "Still waters run deep."

Dad was swell too. He worked his head off Saturday afternoon when he got home from the candy factory, steel-woolling and waxing the old oak floors. Then he shone them up with the long-handled lead polisher that always put me in mind of a giant's toothbrush. I couldn't get over all the fuss that was being made for my fifteenth birthday.

"I don't remember getting all this special attention on my birthday," remarked Arthur. "How come she rates?"

"'Cause Bea's nicer nor you!" piped up Billy.

"She is not!" argued Jakey. Honestly, those two were always bickering about something. They made Arthur and me seem like friends. And they nearly drove Mum crazy.

I spent hours getting myself ready. I washed my hair with real shampoo. Willa bought real shampoo now that she was working steady. She said no amount of rainwater would rinse out Sunlight soap.

"Don't use more than one capful!" she called through the bathroom door.

"I won't!" I promised as I measured out the second capful.

After I rubbed my hair dry, Willa offered to curl it for me with her new curling tongs. She felt a strand between her fingers. "It's too damp," she said. "Go stick your head in the oven."

"That's a terrific idea!" grinned Arthur.

"Arthur" — Mum was up to her elbows in suds in the kitchen sink — "unless you want to be put to work, you'd better make yourself scarce."

"Boy, am I ever glad I'm naturally good-looking," he crowed as he went out the door laughing.

I didn't think his joke was particularly funny because it was true. We looked a lot alike, but by some quirky trick of fate Arthur had turned out smoother than me.

Willa had the curling tongs heating in the blue flame of the gas jet. I pulled my head out of the oven for a breather and saw them turning orangey-red.

"Oh, ye gods, Willa. Don't burn me!"

"Be quiet!" she ordered. Then she took a folded page of newspaper, clamped it between the tongs and held it tight until it smoked. Releasing her grip, she examined the scorched, curled paper. "Too hot," she decided. She blew on the tongs for a few seconds until the glow began to fade, then tested them again. "That's better," she said. "Now hold still."

I closed my eyes and didn't move a muscle. Just then Dad came in with a handful of table knives. He'd cleaned the rust off them by running the blades in and out of the earth, and now he handed them to Mum to wash.

Sniffing suspiciously, he said, "Something's burning!" Dad had a terrible fear of fire ever since he saw a house burned to the ground when he was a boy. We all knew the gruesome story of how Hannibal Hobbs had come screaming out of the inferno, a flaming torch, and thrown himself into a snowbank. For the rest of his life he wore a perfect line down the middle of his body, from head to toe. One half of him was scarred beyond recognition; the other half was handsome as the day is long.

"It's only Bea's hair," Willa explained, and Dad sighed with relief.

The whole curling operation took about half an

hour. "Go look at yourself," Willa said when she'd finished. She was a person of few words.

I looked in the mottled mirror hanging over the kitchen sink and was thrilled to death. My hair was parted in the middle and curled under all the way around in the very latest style.

"Oh, gee, thanks, Willa."

"Well, don't say I never did anything for you." She couldn't help smiling at her own handiwork.

4

The party's over!

By seven o'clock I was ready. I thought I looked pretty good. I was wearing a red crepe de Chine dress, my birthday present from Mum and Dad. It was the first dress I ever owned that Mum hadn't made out of a remnant. Willa had given me a red lipstick to match. It was the reddest I'd ever dared to use and Dad said it looked as if I'd cut my mouth. But he didn't make me wash it off.

Glad and Ruth and Ada arrived together. They looked swell too. Then a bunch of boys arrived, including Georgie Dunn. I still liked Georgie — who wouldn't, with those sparkly eyes and that mischievous grin — but I didn't consider him my boyfriend anymore, mainly because he was always hanging around a girl in third form named Wanda Backhouse. She was really cute and she had a nice neat nose, so I was extra glad that she had such a terrible name. She pronounced it "Backus" but it didn't fool anybody.

The last guests to arrive were Gloria Carlyle and Lorne Huntley.

"Lorne walked me all the way here and he's

promised to walk me home," Gloria told me as I took her upstairs to leave her coat on the bed.

Mum had worked extra hard making new curtains and a matching bedspread especially for this occasion, so when I saw Gloria's eyes taking everything in I was expecting a compliment. But it didn't come. Instead she said, "Who's room is this?"

"My sister's and mine."

"Where do all your brothers sleep?" The way she said it, you'd think there were ten of them.

"In the big front room," I answered defensively.

"My brother and sister and I each have our own room," she said. Then she laid her grey fur coat on our new spread and sidled out the door.

Suddenly our house seemed shabby. I noticed worn brown spots on the hall runner, water marks in the corner of the high ceiling and broken edges along the rubber stair treads. I wished I hadn't asked Gloria.

Arthur already had the radio tuned in to a staticky station. He and Ada started dancing, then Georgie asked me. I wasn't a very good dancer, but since it was my birthday all the boys were obliged to ask me, so at least I wouldn't be a wallflower.

Mum and Dad stayed in the kitchen with the door ajar. I was hoping that being stuck together like that wouldn't start getting on their nerves, because if it did, a fight was sure to erupt. Aunt Ida, Dad's prissy sister, always said with a sniff that Mum and Dad were about as compatible as a cat and dog. She should talk. She and Uncle Wilber were always disgracing the family by getting separated. Anyway, tonight the kitchen remained peaceful.

Willa had gone to the show with Wesley Armstrong, her steady beau, to see *Rose Marie*. At least *he* thought he was her steady beau. Willa said nobody was. She was very independent.

A soft pink light shone from under the rose-coloured fringe of the lamp shade. It was only a 40-watt bulb, so it was very romantic. And when the band played "This Can't Be Love," Lorne asked me to dance!

An hour or so later Mum suddenly opened the door and switched on the ceiling light. All the dancers, who had been snuggling cheek to cheek, jumped apart as if stung by bees.

"Refreshments!" Mum announced cheerily.

After the sandwiches and tarts, Dad brought the lighted cake in and Mum carried the steaming teapot. I made an impossible wish (about Lorne Huntley), then managed to blow all the candles out at once. Everyone cheered and began singing "Happy Birthday." After they'd finished, I opened the presents.

Glad and Ruth and Ada had gone together and bought me a real leather-bound diary with a lock and key and my name embossed in gold on the cover. I was thrilled to pieces. I also got hankies and gloves and two pairs of real silk stockings. Willa hadn't noticed the snag in her best pair yet, so now I could replace them and get away scot-free! Lorne Huntley asked Ruth to relay his present, a box of chocolate-covered cherries, my favourite. I couldn't get over his shyness because at school he acted like he was cock of the walk.

Gloria had saved her gift until last, when she

was sure everybody was watching. Then she handed me a beautifully wrapped oblong package. It felt like a book. It was — an autographed first edition of L.M. Montgomery's latest novel, *Jane of Lantern Hill*. A few weeks before I would have given my right arm for that book, but now it just reminded me of my impossible dream and I couldn't keep the pained look off my face. I didn't even trust myself to speak.

"Well," she snapped impatiently, "don't you like it?"

"Oh, sure," was all I could manage to say.

"Well, that's gratitude for you!" Turning on her heel, her full skirt swirling, she flounced into the front room.

Someone turned off the overhead light again and Mum went back to the kitchen. I heard Dad say he was going down to the cellar to half-sole Jakey's leaky shoes. Good, I thought, that'll keep him busy so they won't fight.

The band began to play a real oldie, one I'd often heard Mum sing: "When Frances dances with me ... holy gee!" Mum got a kick out of that song because her name was Frances. I was just beginning to enjoy myself with a boy named Victor Barnes, who made dancing seem easy, when a loud commotion started in the front room.

Mum ran in and switched on the light just in time to see Lorne Huntley punch Georgie Dunn right in the mouth. Georgie went sprawling across Dad's slippery floor, knocking over the floor lamp and smashing it to pieces.

In the rumpus that followed, a dish of blue grapes got knocked off the table with a resounding crash.

The fruit flew all over, squashing and splattering everywhere. Arthur, who came charging to help Georgie, slid on them and bowled Ada right off her feet. Sitting among the grapes, her new white dress splotched with purple juice, she started to cry.

"What's going on here?" The racket had brought Dad running up from the cellar.

"He started it, Mr. Thomson." Everybody, including myself, pointed accusingly at Lorne Huntley. When the chips were down, our gang on Veeny Street stuck together.

"I'm sorry, Mr. Thomson," simpered Gloria, reaching out and clutching Dad's arm. "I'm afraid it's all my fault. The boys were fighting over whose turn it was to dance with me. I *told* them they'd both get a chance but they wouldn't listen."

Even Dad, who had a volatile temper, simmered down under her spell. "No harm done," he muttered gruffly.

But Mum was livid. "No harm, my foot!" she screeched, glaring at Gloria with flashing black eyes. "Maybe *your* mother doesn't have to worry about where to get another floor lamp, but I do!" In a frenzy she started grabbing up the broken pieces. "Get your coats on, all of you. The party's over."

In five minutes flat everybody had cleared out except Glad and Ruth. Poor Ada had gone home to soak her new white dress in vinegar and water.

"We'll stay and help clean up, Cousin Fran," said Ruth nervously. She and Glad started picking up grapes.

I thought I'd never forgive Mum for embarrassing me like that. How could I ever face my friends again? Especially Lorne Huntley. What would he and Gloria be saying on their way back to their classy neighbourhoods?

Complaining bitterly, Mum swept the mess up into the dustpan. Dad began grimly wiping grapestains and bloodstains off the floor he'd worked so hard on. We girls stood around not knowing what to do next. Mum and Dad stopped grumbling, but the air was tense. Sometimes upsets like that were all it took to start a full-blown fight between them.

I was expecting that to happen any second when a ghostly voice drifted down from above. "What's going on down there?" We all looked up to see Billy's impish face framed in the stovepipe hole. The sight made everybody laugh and the tension was broken.

Then Willa yelled up at him, "You get out of my room, Billy!" She and Wesley had come in the kitchen door unnoticed. Quick as a wink Billy's face disappeared and we heard him padding barefoot down the hall.

"What happened?" asked Willa, staring at the shattered lamp.

"The less said the better," muttered Mum. So Willa told Wesley he'd better go, which was a perfect excuse not to have to kiss him goodnight in the hallway. Poor Wesley. I felt sorry for him.

"I guess we'd better go too," said Glad uneasily.

"Thank you, girls," said Mum breathlessly, her hand over her heart. Then she added, "There's no friends like old friends."

Ignoring that remark, I gathered up my presents and stomped upstairs. Throwing Gloria's gift on the closet shelf, I stuffed the other things into my drawer and opened my new diary.

Inside, in a slot, was a gold pencil. I wrote:

Nov. 9, 1937

Dear Diary,
 Today I am fifteen years old and my life lies in ruins at my feet.

B.M.T.

I locked the diary with the miniature key and looked for a place to hide it. I noticed a knothole in the thick wood baseboard. The key fit neatly in the hole and when the knot was replaced no one would ever know it was there.

5

Three Smart Girls

Between the loss of my "calling" and the loss of a potential boyfriend, I was about ready to take Arthur's advice and stick my head in the oven. Then along came a new idol who changed all that.

Ever since I'd seen my first silent moving picture at the Kingswood in Birchcliff years ago, I'd been mad about movies. So when Glad and Ruth and I went downtown to see a Christmas special called *Three Smart Girls* we could hardly wait to get there. The newspaper ad read: *Scintillating young Canadian soprano, Deanna Durbin, sings her way right into your heart!*

Well, did she ever. She was just fifteen, the perfect age for an idol. And what a fascinating name — Deanna Durbin! It made Gloria Carlyle sound like Zazu Pitts!

As usual, we stopped off on our transfers at Yonge and Bloor to visit the Uptown Nuthouse, my Aunt Susan's store. Poor Aunt Susan, she had so many relatives who just happened to stop by to say hello on their way downtown that she must have given away a hundred pounds of nuts every year.

When we came out of the show two hours later, we blinked in amazement at the bright winter sun.

"I forgot it was still daylight," I said, narrowing my eyes against the sudden brilliance. "I felt as if I was in another world, didn't you?""I was living in the picture," said Glad dreamily. "I felt as if I was one of the three sisters."

"Wasn't it exciting how they rescued their beloved father from that wretched gold digger?" exclaimed Ruth.

"And the family reunion — the father and mother and three daughters together again. Oh, it was magnificent!" As a storyteller, I loved the dramatic, happy ending.

"And the music was simply divine!" added Ruth, who was a born musician herself.

We drifted onto the Yonge streetcar to the tune of "Waltzing in the Clouds" and settled on the round wooden seat at the back.

"I've got a swell idea," said Ruth mysteriously.

"What? Tell us!"

"Let's form an exclusive club called the *Three Smart Girls Club*."

"Terrific!" I agreed.

"What will Ada say?" worried Glad. Ada had a Saturday job now and hadn't been able to come.

"Well, we can't have four smart girls," reasoned Ruth.

"I want to be Deanna Durbin," I said.

"You can't be. Your hair's too fair," said Ruth.

"Then I will!" Glad flashed a smile.

"You can't either. Your hair's too dark," said Ruth, fluffing up her own nut-brown curls.

This is one of Deanna's early picture's, from "Three Smart Girls," with her are Nan Grey (left) and Barbara Read. Deanna surely is growing quickly.

The Three Smart Girls Club

We argued all the way home, then Glad and I had to admit that Ruth, with her Deanna Durbin hairdo (completely accidental) and her round, nice-featured face, actually was the best choice. That left the other two movie sisters to choose from, which was easy because Nan Grey was a blue-eyed blonde, like me, and Barbara Read was a brown-eyed brunette, like Glad.

That night we had our first meeting in Glad's kitchen and drew up the club rules.

The Three Smart Girls Club. Ruth printed the title neatly at the top of a page of foolscap.

Rule 1. Only the three of us can belong because that's what makes it exclusive. That was Ruth's contribution.

Rule 2. We must see every Deanna Durbin movie together if humanly possible. That was mine.

Rule 3. We will buy all Deanna Durbin records and all movie magazines featuring her pictures, and the club will own them collectively. That was Glad's idea, but how we were going to do it I couldn't imagine because we hardly ever had any money.

Rule 4. We will begin a giant scrapbook devoted to our idol's life and fabulous career.

"Anything else?" Ruth tapped the pencil on her front teeth thoughtfully.

"Well, if there are any more rules or regulations they'll have to wait," interposed Aunt Ellie, "because I need the table now."

"Okay. We'll meet here every Saturday night after supper. Is that all right, Mumma?"

"That's just dandy," Aunt Ellie agreed. Then, with Florrie's play dress draped over her arm, she shook her ragbag onto the table and began searching for a patch.

After that we lived from one Deanna Durbin show to the next. Night after night I dreamed that every time I opened my mouth her glorious voice would come soaring out in radiant high C's.

One Saturday during an afternoon meeting of the club Glad's mother interrupted with some exciting news. "Just hearken to this," she said, spreading the weekend newspaper out in front of us on the table. "It says here there's going to be a Deanna Durbin look-alike contest. Maybe Ruth could win it."

The green-eyed monster leaped up in me. It was bad enough that Ruth was the chosen one in our club, but if she actually won a look-alike contest I'd have a bilious attack and die.

"Don't worry," Glad consoled me as we crossed the street Monday morning, watching our step. (The Silverwood's Dairy wagon had just passed by, leaving steaming horsebuns in its wake.) "Ruth probably won't be able to afford film for the camera. And Cousin Aimie probably won't let her use it anyway."

But Glad was wrong. Cousin Aimie did better than that. She was so intrigued with the idea of her daughter winning a famous screen-star contest that she marched Ruth straight down to Paramount Studios on Yonge Street where they had a special on, four poses for a quarter. One of the pictures turned out to be a remarkable likeness.

Although it nearly killed me, I managed to wish Ruth luck. But the results weren't going to be announced until early in the new year. It was going to be a long winter.

6
Cousin Winn

A week before Christmas something happened that distracted me from the contest. Cousin Winnifred came to board with us.

Actually Winn's mother had been our mother's second cousin, so we weren't very closely related, but Mum had a special soft spot for Winn because her mother, Cousin Addie, had died when Winn was only a tyke, three years old. The saddest thing I ever heard Winn say was, "I never knew my mother, but I've missed her all my life." Those sober words, coming from the lighthearted Winn, chilled me to the bone.

Winn had landed herself a swell job in the west end of Toronto in a big food store called Loblaw's Groceteria. Before that she had been a housemaid for a rich family in Birchcliff, in the east end. Her pay there was twenty dollars a month and they only gave her one night off a week. Mum said it was a sin and shame how rich people took advantage of poor girls. But when Winn got hired by Loblaw's she had the last laugh. She left her stingy employers high and dry without any notice so they didn't have a "char" to do their dirty work.

At Loblaw's Groceteria you carried a wicker basket and helped yourself from the shelves. Then you took your purchases up to the cashier. That's who Winn was, the cashier. But Mum still preferred to deal at Hunter's corner store. She liked the friendliness and convenience. If you ran short of anything, even on a Sunday, all you had to do was knock on their back door and they'd cheerfully get you what you wanted. And besides, you could run up a weekly bill at Hunter's. At Loblaw's you had to have cash.

Every Saturday night after the store closed, at eleven, Winn would come home dog-tired and hand Mum six dollars for board, exactly the same as Willa. Mum said we'd soon be on Easy Street. She even told me she was thinking of opening a bank account — imagine! — in hopes of saving enough money to buy the house on Veeny Street. But she swore me to secrecy.

*   *   *

We had a swell Christmas that year. The best ever. Jakey got a Big Ben pocket watch and all day long he went around asking, "Does anybody want to know what time it is?" Santa had brought Billy a wind-up train that kept him spellbound the entire day. And Dad even bought Mum a present — a two-slice Waverley toaster. She was pleased as punch. I don't remember him ever buying her a present before.

Willa and Winn went together and bought me a powder blue blouse. Mum and Dad gave me a pleated flannel skirt. "Now all I need is saddle shoes," I said. Gloria had saddle shoes.

"You can't expect to get everything at once," Mum pointed out.

Later in the day, to my astonishment, Lorne Huntley came to the door with a box of chocolates (cherry centres again), and because it was Christmas Day Dad let him step inside the hall. So that made my day perfect.

Wesley Armstrong gave Willa a tapered blue bottle of Evening in Paris perfume. "Boy, oh boy," teased Winn, "he's sure a-courtin' you, Willa." Willa never let on she heard, but her cheeks turned pink.

"I'll trade you my cherry centres for your perfume, Willa," I said, tempting her with a sample. If she agreed I could pretend that Lorne had given me the perfume, which was much more romantic than cherry centres. But she just said, "You've got hopes," popped the sample into her mouth and went away laughing.

We had a beautiful big turkey for Christmas dinner. Usually Aunt Aggie, Dad's sister in Muskoka, sent us a chicken through the mail. Sure enough, it arrived right on time, so Mum saved it for New Year's. She tied it in a potato sack and hung it on the clothesline. Then Dad propped up the line with a pole. The chicken froze solid and was perfectly preserved a week later.

Having Winnifred for Christmas made a real difference. For one thing Mum and Dad tried not to fight in front of her. Also, Winn was more fun than a barrel of monkeys. She always had a joke or a trick to play on somebody.

"I stuck up for you last night, Arthur," she said in a serious voice as she helped herself to more dressing.

"You did?" Arthur fell for it hook, line and sinker.

"Sure did!" Winn's blue eyes were twinkling. "Do you know a girl named Marjorie Tabbs?"

"Yeah." Arthur coloured up. He had a crush on Marjorie Tabbs, who was in fifth form and wouldn't give him the time of day. "What about it?"

"Well . . ." Winn paused so long, twirling her fork in the air, that we all stopped eating to listen. "Marjorie said that you weren't fit to eat with pigs . . . and I said you were!"

For a split second there was dead silence. Then we all roared with laughter.

"I owe you one, Winn!" grinned red-faced Arthur. One thing I'll say for my brother, he could take a joke on himself.

"Oh, Winn" — Mum was wiping the tears from her cheeks — "you're your mother all over again. Addie was always the life of the party." Then she began to laugh and cry at once, remembering her long-dead friend. I laughed so hard myself I had to leave the table to go to the bathroom.

"Bea," Billy said with a puzzled frown when I came back and sat down beside him, "will you understand it for me?"

His funny little question set us all off again. "I'll try, Billy, but Winn's jokes are kind of hard to explain."

"I understand it," said smart-aleck Jakey. "I'll explain it to you later, Bill." (Bill!) He took his watch out of his pocket and studied it importantly. "I'll explain it to you at seven o'clock," he promised. That started us laughing all over again. I can't remember when we were all so happy at the dinner table.

That night I wrote in my diary:

Dear Diary,

Christmas was fun this year! I hope Winn stays forever, even though I hate sleeping three in a bed. She and Willa make me sleep in the middle and sometimes I wake up actually gasping for air. And they think it's funny! Also they say I talk in my sleep and answer all their questions, so now they know all my secrets. I could kill them for that! But I still hope Winn stays. I think she's going to bring us good luck in the new year. l938, imagine! Time sure flies. Mum says if time begins to fly it means you're getting old. Well, I'm in my sixteenth year so, as Aunt Aggie would say, I'm "no spring chicken anymore!"

B.M.T.

Locking the diary, I hid the key in the knothole. Then I tried to get to sleep before Winn and Willa came to bed and smothered me again.

7
My first job

Both Glad and Ruth had been lucky enough to get
Deanna Durbin dresses for Christmas. But no matter
how hard I pleaded Mum said she simply couldn't
afford a new dress for me right now and I'd have to
earn it myself.

I had been trying for months to get a job after
school, without success. Then one day Ada-May said
she was quitting her baby-minding job because she'd
finally been taken on steady at Stedman's Department Store. She recommended me for her old job —
and I got it.

New Year's Eve was my first night. "Be here
sharp at seven o'clock," said Mrs. Bosley over the
telephone.

"Yes, Mrs. Bosley," I answered politely. Ada
called her Mrs. Bossy — because she was! — but she
warned me never to let it slip out of my mouth.

I got there on the dot of seven to find a sinkful of
dirty dishes and the twins running around still
dressed in their Little Lord Fauntleroy suits.

"Now do the dishes first" — Mrs. Bosley started
right in giving me orders — "and be extra careful how

you handle my precious stemware." Stemware? "It was a wedding present from my Great-Aunt Emma in England and is practically priceless." That's how she talked, to show off. "Mind you keep a sharp eye on the boys while you're doing the washing up. And be sure you put all the tableware in the right cupboards. The good dishes go in the sideboard and the glassware goes in the china cabinet." The glassware must be the stemware, I thought.

"After that you may bathe the twins together in the same tub, but be sure you wash Gaylord's hair and not Gaston's. He's got the sniffles. In case you can't tell them apart — the darlings even fool me sometimes — Gaylord is the one with flecks of brown in the blue of his left eye. It's an inherited trait from his father's side. All my family have pure blue eyes.

"When you get them into their sleepers — Gaylord's are yellow and Gaston's are blue, I've already laid them out on their beds to save you trouble — they may stay up for exactly half an hour, not a minute longer, to listen to our Philco. I shall depend on your integrity to choose a fitting program for their young ears. I don't want them to hear any slang or indelicate words.

"After you put them to bed and hear their prayers you may listen to the radio yourself for an hour as a special New Year's Eve treat. You should enjoy that because I'm sure you don't have a radio in your house. Now, are there any questions, Beatrice?"

"No, Mrs. Bossy," I answered without thinking. "But we do have a radio — a DeForest Cro—"

"What did you call me?"

Good grief, it had slipped out. "Oh, I'm sorry. I meant to say *Bosley.* You see, I have this slight impediment in my speech. The doctor says it's nothing to worry about. It's just that I was born with too short a tongue." Actually I had an extra long tongue that I could dart out like an anteater and touch the end of my nose with. But at least she seemed to accept my excuse.

The minute their parents went out the door those two little "darlings" changed into devilish imps. I knew I'd never be able to handle them and the stemware together, so I decided to get rid of them first.

I dragged them, kicking and screaming, up the stairs and threw them into the bathtub together.

"Which one of you is Gaylord?" I demanded, peering into their identical faces, trying to find the brown specks in one blue eye.

"Me! Me!" they squealed in unison.

"All right, I'll give you one more chance." I used a really mad voice. "Which one is Gaston?"

"I am! I am!" they said gleefully. So without another word I shoved both their curly heads under water. Up they came, spluttering and shrieking and calling me terrible names.

At last I got the twins into their sleepers and sat them down side by side on the chesterfield. In the time it took me to tune in the radio they had started a real cat-and-dog fight. I squeezed myself between them and pinned their arms to their sides so they couldn't move a muscle.

A ghost story was just beginning on CFCA. It scared the daylights out of them and when it was over they ran up to bed, covered their heads and wouldn't even come out to say their prayers. I never heard another peep all night.

At last I got around to tackling the mountain of

dishes. By the time I was done I was worn to a frazzle. It was almost midnight when I turned the radio on again. I just managed to catch the tail end of Guy Lombardo's band playing "Auld Lang Syne" before I fell fast asleep on the soft velour chesterfield.

The radio was still crackling when the Bosleys arrived home at two. Mr. Bosley was in a good mood, singing loudly, "It's shree o'clock in the morning . . . we've danched the whole night shroo . . ." But Mrs. Bosley was fit to be tied. "How dare you fall asleep!" How dare I? I was so tired after all that work that I couldn't stay awake. And I hadn't broken a single piece of stemware either. "My precious babies could have been murdered in their beds!" Who'd want to murder them? I wondered. Except me. "And the radio still blaring, wasting electricity when the station has long been off the air."

She clicked off the radio (which was crackling, not blaring), snapped open her purse (evening bag, she called it) and slapped a quarter and a dime into my hand.

"I had fully intended giving you fifty cents, since it's New Year's Eve, but considering your negligence there'll be no gratuities for you, my girl!" (Her girl, my foot!)

By the time I got my coat and galoshes on, Mr. Bosley had his off. His nose was red and he yawned hugely as he chucked me under the chin. "Happy New Year's, wushyername," he slurred, then went stumbling up the stairs.

"Now you go straight home," ordered Mrs. Bosley as she shoved me out the door.

"Where else would I go?" I muttered into my scarf. There was no place I'd rather be than safe and warm in bed beside my sister.

The night was pitch-black, freezing cold and eerily quiet. Mayberry Hill seemed like a mountain as I trudged up it to Windermere Avenue. From the top of the hill I could look down the street and see Grampa Cole's old cement-block house. I stopped for a second, wishing I had the nerve to take the shortcut through his yard and across the lane to ours. If he'd still been alive I might have. It was more than a year now since he'd "gone home," as Mum put it. "Oh, Grampa," I mourned, missing him for the thousandth time. But I knew the back lane would be as dark as a graveyard, and at least there were a few lights on the street.

Just at that moment I saw the figure of a man come creeping out of Grampa's laneway. As soon as he spotted me under the lamp-post he started running toward me. Terrified, I flew along Mayberry and down Veeny Street, my screams piercing the air like flying icicles.

I could hear loud yelling and pounding feet closing in behind me.

Our house was in total darkness. That meant the front door was locked and I'd have to go through the black alleyway between the houses. He'd catch me for sure in the alleyway. He'd kill me in the alleyway! A picture of my frozen, bloodstained body flashed through my mind. Who would make the grisly discovery in the morning? I wondered.

Suddenly, across the road, Aunt Ellie's light

flashed on. She must have heard my screams, because the door flew open just as I came stumbling through it.

"A man! A man!" I shrieked hysterically. Shoving me inside, she stepped fearlessly out the door in her kimono. And there was the man, panting like a runaway horse, his greatcoat flying in the wind. My dad! My very own dad!

"Jim!" cried Aunt Ellie. "It's yourself! For mercy sakes, you nearly scared Bea half to death."

"You foolish girl!" Dad yelled, pulling me roughly into his arms. "Didn't you hear me calling you?"

"Oh, Dad!" It had been a long time since I'd felt the comfort of his old khaki coat. "Am I ever glad it's you!"

"I'm sorry I gave you such a fright, Ellie," he apologized over my shoulder. "What in thunder are you doing up at this hour?"

"I came down to boil an onion," explained Aunt Ellie. "Our Florrie's got the earache again. Well, all's well that ends well, Jim. See you tomorrow."

"Much obliged, Ellie. I hope Florrie gets relief."

Aunt Ellie nodded her head wearily as she latched the door behind us.

Mum was sitting in the kitchen with her feet up on the oven door, an open book on her lap. It was *Anne's House of Dreams.* Funny how you notice things like that in a crisis.

"It's a good thing you sent me after her," Dad said. "She was let walk home all alone."

"You mean to say" — Mum sprang to her feet and the book flopped on the floor — "that Mr. Bosley allowed you to walk all the way home alone at this ungodly hour?"

"I think he intended to walk me home, Mum." I had a feeling this whole affair was going to end up to my disadvantage. Besides, I kind of liked Mr. Bosley. "But he was a bit drunk. His nose was all red and he sort of staggered up the stairs."

"Well, he can just stagger right down again." Sparks of outrage flew from Mum's dark eyes. Going straight to the phone on the dining room wall, she dialled Bosleys' number furiously. It must have rung at least a dozen times.

"Let me speak to *Mr.* Bosley," Mum demanded. Then she said, "Well, wake him up if you don't want the police at your door."

The threat worked and presently Mr. Bosley came on the line. "This is Beatrice Thomson's mother." Mum's voice quivered with anger. He must have said he'd never heard tell of me because all of a sudden my mother — my God-fearing, church-going mother — started swearing a blue streak. Then, when she got that out of her system, she said, "My girl could have been attacked coming home alone tonight. And if anything had happened to her I'd have gone for you myself!" With that she slammed the receiver down, with a fierce jangle, in his ear.

Needless to say, I never minded Gaylord and Gaston again. I never got my Deanna Durbin dress either. What's more, when the school nurse weighed me on the first day in the new year she found I had lost five pounds. So I guess that's what's known as being scared skinny — literally!

8
We, the undersigned

At long last the big day came when the winner of the look-alike contest was to be announced. Glad and Ruth and I congregated anxiously at Ruth's front-room window waiting for the paperboy.

"Here he comes!" I spotted him about ten houses up the street on the other side.

"I'll run to meet him!" cried Glad.

"You'll catch your death without your sweater-coat!" called Cousin Aimie after her. But Glad flew recklessly out the door, leaving it wide open. The wind nearly blew it off its hinges. Cousin Aimie yelled, "For mercy sakes!" and jumped up to shut it. Ruth stood still as a statue, her face ghostly white.

Back came Glad, bursting through the door, the cold air rushing in behind her. "For mercy sakes!" cried Cousin Aimie, jumping up to shut it again.

Tingling with suspense, we scattered the paper all over the floor. We found the picture — but it wasn't Ruth. It was a girl who looked so much like Deanna Durbin that she could have been the famous soprano's twin sister.

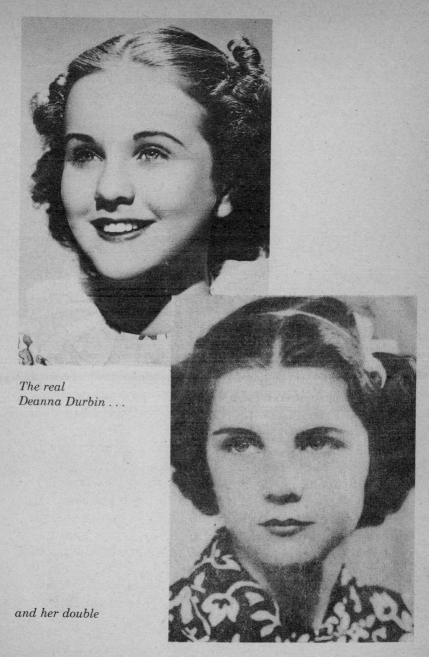

*The real
Deanna Durbin . . .*

and her double

Big tears gathered in Ruth's eyes and spilled onto the picture, spreading in damp grey blots. Suddenly I was glad I hadn't had a chance in the contest. At least I was spared the agony of losing.

"Never mind, Ruthie." Even as I consoled her I felt a surge of relief inside me. "You're prettier than her anyway." It was a lie, of course, but at least it was a white lie.

"Yeah!" agreed Glad. "And I'll bet anything she can't play the piano half as well as you can." Ruth had perfect pitch. She could play absolutely anything by ear. She had heard Deanna sing "I Love to Whistle" only once, in the movie *Mad about Music*, and she could play it perfectly right straight through.

But Ruth was inconsolable.

"I think it's time you girls forgot about moving picture stars and got at your homework," said her mother, trying vainly to hide her own disappointment.

Glad and I didn't see Ruth for weeks after that. Then one day she met us after school and told us some very disturbing news. It seemed that Deanna Durbin's Canadian look-alike had sent an autographed copy of her prize-winning photograph to the famous actress and it hadn't even been acknowledged, let alone answered in kind.

Immediately we called an emergency meeting of the Three Smart Girls Club.

"What shall we do about it?" asked Ruth.

"Well, it's an insult to all Canadians," I said in righteous indignation. "After all, she *is* a Canadian."

"Was," corrected Glad. "I read she's an American now."

"Just the same," said Ruth, "I think it's our duty as members of her fan club to write her a letter of protest."

The suggestion was passed unanimously. Glad contributed the pen, paper and four-cent stamp. Ruth wrote the letter because her penmanship was the neatest (and also, she was the injured party) and I dictated the words because I was the best at composition.

> *16, 17, 18 Veeny Street,*
> *Swansea, Ontario, Canada,*
> *March 17, 1938.*

Dear Deanna,

Let us begin by stating that we, the undersigned, are probably your most avid fans on the face of this earth. In fact we have formed an exclusive club appropriately named the Three Smart Girls Club in honour of your grand and glorious pictures. It is our considered opinion that you are the finest soprano in the world today. Together we have assembled a giant scrapbook filled with photos and articles about your life and sparkling career.

Therefore it grieves us deeply to have to find fault with you in any way. However, it has come to our attention that the winner of your Canadian look-alike contest (who, by the way, is a complete stranger to us) sent her prize-winning, autographed photograph to you and it was completely ignored.

However, we the undersigned feel that this can only be an oversight on your part because your obvious sweet nature (which is apparent in all your films), as well as the fact that you are a Canadian by birth, would never allow you to be so thoughtless and cruel.

Therefore we beg of you, on behalf of Toronto's look-alike, to rectify this error as soon as possible.

We, the undersigned, will remain forever your faithful and devoted fans.

> *Ruth Aimie Vaughan,*
> *Gladys Pearl Cole,*
> *and Beatrice Myrtle Thomson.*

We addressed the envelope c/o Universal Studios, Hollywood, California, United States of America, and dropped it in the mailbox on our way to school the next morning.

Time passed and the letter was forced to the back of our minds by the awful throes of Easter examinations. Then a few weeks later the three of us were sauntering down Veeny Street sharing a bag of humbugs when we saw Ruth's mother standing on their front stoop waving something high in the air. She looked really excited, so we broke into a run.

In her hand she held a flat parcel about ten inches square. "Look at the postmark!" she cried when we reached her.

"Oh, my gosh!" Ruth squealed. "It's from Hollywood!"

Screaming like magpies, we tore open the package. Inside was an absolutely gorgeous coloured photograph of our idol. A typewritten letter was enclosed explaining that the exact same portrait had been sent to Canada's look-alike with profound apologies.

A bit of brown wrapping paper still clung to the bottom of the picture frame. Ruth ripped it off and there in the lower right-hand corner, in the star's own handwriting, were the words *To Ruth Aimie*

Vaughan and Gladys Pearl Cole, with all my very best wishes, Deanna Durbin.

My name was conspicuously absent. Frantically we turned the picture over. But it wasn't on the back either. My heart fluttered and seemed to stop and I thought I was going to drop dead. Bursting into tears, I bolted out the back door, leaped across the alleyway that separated our houses and went crashing into our kitchen, scaring the wits out of Mum.

"Booky!" She always reverted to my nickname when she was frightened. "What in the name of heaven is the matter?"

I sobbed out the whole awful story.

"Oh, pshaw, Bea." Mum sounded relieved. "Nobody ever died of envy, you know." That made me cry all the harder. Then, when she realized the depths of my despair, she added quickly, "Why don't you sit yourself down and write Deanna a nice letter explaining the oversight? I'm sure it's all a big mistake."

Her advice gave me a glimmer of hope. Immediately I composed another letter and mailed it secretly. I didn't want the other two "smart girls" to know until I had the autographed photograph right in my hands.

For months and months I waited, sometimes going up the street to meet the mailman, until at last I had to accept the fact that I was never going to hear a word from Deanna Durbin.

Oddly, I didn't blame *her*. Willa had told me that sometimes famous movie queens had jealous secretaries who threw away fan letters if they were too thrillingly complimentary (which mine was), and the star herself never knew a thing about it.

I was convinced that this was what had happened. So my loyalty to my idol remained untarnished, but I never told Glad or Ruth about it. And I never really got over it.

9
The Pally

By the time spring came and the weather turned warm and balmy I was sick to death of my Christmas outfit. Every other night I had to wash and iron my blue blouse and Mum sponged and pressed my grey flannel skirt.

"If only you weren't so skinny, Bea," Mum complained, "you could grow into Winn's and Willa's things."

One morning as I was getting my clean blouse out of the closet I noticed Willa's new one hanging there invitingly. It was peach-coloured with long, full sleeves and a ruffled neckline. It was absolutely irresistible.

"She'll kill you when she finds out, Bea," Glad said, shifting her load of books from one hip to the other as we trekked up Jane Street.

"No, she won't, because I get home before her and I'll be sure to hang it in the same place at the end of the closet."

"Which end — left or right?"

"Right. I think. Darn you, Glad, now you've got me worried."

The blouse was a mile too big, so I got Glad to pin it at the back in the school washroom. Also the shoulder seams hung too low, so I had to thrust my shoulders back, which did wonders for my skinny figure. Across my forehead and in front of my ears I had set sugar-water kiss curls. The curls combed out a bit crispy, but not too bad. The peach-coloured georgette blouse seemed to brighten up my complexion (I was sallow when I wasn't suntanned), and even my eyes looked bluer. For once I was halfways satisfied with myself.

At lunch time in the basement cafeteria I was carefully eating my meatloaf sandwich so as not to let the homemade mustard drip onto Willa's blouse, when all of a sudden Glad got up and vanished. Lorne Huntley took her place. He straddled the bench, drinking from a big bottle of Kik Cola.

"How's tricks?" he asked, as friendly as anything, just as if he hadn't been ignoring me for months. Everybody knew that he and Gloria Carlyle were keeping company. "Want a sip?" He bent the soggy paper straw towards me.

"No thanks." I was going around with Georgie again, so even though my heart was racing a mile a minute, I decided to act choosy.

"I'll get a new straw," he said, and before I could stop him he went leapfrogging over the rows of tables and brought back a fresh straw. So I took a sip.

"You busy Friday night?" he asked.

"Maybe," I hedged, facing him squarely so he wouldn't notice my knobby nose. Was I glad I'd had the nerve to wear Willa's blouse! "Georgie Dunn usually comes over."

"How's about going dancing with me at the Pally?"

The Pally! That was short for the Palais Royale and going there was beyond my wildest hopes. Besides, I was a terrible dancer. Sometimes Arthur and I tried out a few steps, but Arthur always said he might as well be dancing with the floor mop. Outside of that and my disastrous birthday party I hadn't had much practice.

"I'll have to ask my mum," I said, knowing I sounded like a ninny, but needing time to think.

"Okey-doke. I'll call you Thursday." He winked one beautiful eye and went bounding away.

Instantly "bunch" (that's what we girls who hung around together had dubbed ourselves — not "the bunch" or "our bunch," just bunch) popped up from all directions.

"What did Lorne want?" Glad asked, her gleaming eyes following his tall figure as he went loping, two steps at a time, up the cement staircase.

"He invited me to the Pally on Friday night," I said, trying to sound casual.

"Oh, wow!" exclaimed Wanda Backhouse.

"Talk about luck!" Jane LaRose stared at me as if I had a four-leaf clover stuck to my forehead.

"What did you say?" persisted Glad.

"I said I'd let him know Thursday."

"You're kidding!" cried Glad.

"Oh, wow!" crowed Wanda again. She was definitely the dumbest member of "bunch." No wonder Georgie had gotten bored with her.

Speaking of dumb, I didn't learn a thing that afternoon. Math gave me enough trouble without having Lorne on my mind. But I did manage to remember, when I got home, to hang Willa's blouse up exactly where I'd found it.

Thursday night the phone rang. Winn and Willa and I all jumped for it at once, but Willa grabbed it first. Then she handed it to me. "You're always on the phone," she grumbled. That was true. Mum said I had phone-itis. I'd no sooner say goodbye to Glad at the front than I'd go straight in and phone her. I couldn't get over the thrill of having a phone of our own at last. But this time I didn't talk long. What can you say to a boy when there are four big ears listening in?

When Lorne picked me up on Friday he was dressed fit to kill in a blue serge suit with a felt fedora to match. He was the only boy I knew who owned a fedora.

I was wearing my birthday dress, which Mum had let out to fit. Willa had done my hair with the tongs again, and Winn said I could borrow her new string of beads as a finishing touch. Mum insisted that I wear my threadbare spring coat because it was bound to be chilly down by the lake.

She and Dad weren't too happy about my date. "I'll never forget that boy's performance at your party," Mum said skeptically.

Arthur looked up from his artwork and said, "Aw, it wasn't any more his fault than mine and Georgie's."

That seemed to mollify Mum and Dad. "Thanks, Arthur," I said.

"You're welcome, Bea." He grinned. We were getting positively civil to each other.

Lorne and I walked along the boardwalk holding

hands, but not talking much. Lake Ontario glittered like gold in the setting sun. Soft waves lapped on the sand of Sunnyside Beach. The amusement park was open and we could hear wild screams coming from atop the roller coaster. I don't remember ever feeling so thrilled and happy before.

Sweet music floated out of the open Pally doors. The electric sign above read: *Bert Niosi, Canada's King of Swing!* A notice tacked to the door said: *Ten cents a dance.* Lorne jingled a pocketful of dimes.

The dance floor was crowded already and the band was playing "Love in Bloom." Lorne slipped his arm around my waist, under my coat, and swung me around the huge ballroom. A fresh lake breeze blew in the open doors at the back, ruffling our hair. I was in seventh heaven!

A little while later, as we danced by the bandstand, Lorne called out to the dapper man with the baton, "Hey, Bert, how about 'Smoke Gets in Your Eyes'?"

The band leader winked and nodded without missing a beat. Sure enough, the next piece he played was "Smoke Gets in Your Eyes."

"Do you actually *know* Bert Niosi?" I asked, flabbergasted.

Lorne shrugged nonchalantly. "He's a friend of the family."

"Oh, wow!" I cried, sounding just like Wanda. Wait till I tell bunch about this! I thought.

It was a wonderful evening. We danced to "Always" and "Carolina Moon," and every time I tripped over Lorne's feet he apologized and said it was all his fault. Afterwards we went to the amusement park and had a terrifying ride on the roller coaster. Then we shared a paper cone of vinegar and chips. Finally we headed up Ellis Avenue, our arms around each other under a star-spangled sky. Fireflies blinked their lights all over Grenadier Pond. It was a magical sight.

Home again, we sat on my front stoop and kissed four times. Everything would have been fine if I'd said goodnight right then and gone in. But Lorne pulled a five-cent packet of Turrets out of his shirt pocket, and scratching a match alight with his thumbnail, very romantically lit two cigarettes at once.

It was my first cigarette and I didn't know how to hold it. "Pinch it between your thumb and finger and take a big drag and swallow it. Then let it out real slow, like this." He demonstrated, drawing in deeply. Then he formed his lips into a circle and blew a halo right over my head. It dissolved in the soft night air.

Laughing, I tried to copy him and instantly went into an uncontrollable coughing fit. The awful racket I made, choking and gagging, brought my dad running to the door. He took one look and erupted like a volcano. In two quick motions he smacked the cigarette out of my mouth and kicked Lorne down the steps. Lorne landed on his feet, like a cat, the cigarette still clamped between his handsome lips.

"You," Dad snarled at me, his pale eyes smouldering, "get yourself inside! And you, boy, get out of my sight before I take my belt to you!"

"Help, Mum!" I screamed. I was really scared of Dad when his eyes changed from blue to grey. Mum came flying from the kitchen. At first she put her arm protectively around me. But when she heard the story she angrily ordered me to bed.

Embarrassed by Dad and feeling betrayed by Mum, I burst into sobs and went racing up the stairs.

Winn was away visiting one of her brothers, so Willa and I had the bed to ourselves. I thought she was asleep, so I stifled my sobs and crept miserably in beside her. Then she did the most extraordinary thing. Willa, who never touched anybody if she could help it, actually patted my back. "Never mind, Bea," she comforted me. "I know exactly how you feel. Only it was even worse for me when I was your age because I was the oldest and they always expected me to be perfect."

"I guess it's worse for Arthur too, then," I sniffled, "since he's two years older than me." I hoped it was, because misery loves company.

"No," Willa dashed my hopes. "He's a boy. Boys get away with murder." She gave my back a final pat, more like a slap, and added sternly, "But don't you dare start smoking or I'll make you sleep on the floor. You reek!"

With that she turned over and got as far away from me as possible, and that was the end of our discussion. It wasn't much, but it was the first time my sister and I had had a heart-to-heart talk. So, as Aunt Milly would say, "Things are never so bad they couldn't be worse" — or one of those old sayings.

The next day I wrote the whole episode up in my diary, and when I read it over it sounded for all the world like a page out of *True Romances*.

10
Aunt Milly

On Sunday Willa got her peach blouse out of the closet to wear to church. Instantly she spotted the soiled collar. "You dirty rat!" she screeched. That was the worst thing Willa ever called anybody, a rat, but I'd never heard her use the adjective before. She chose another blouse and glared at me all through church.

That afternoon she washed the blouse in the kitchen basin and hung it out to dry. Later, when she went to iron it, she was so busy bawling me out that she forgot to wet her finger to test the iron so she scorched the blouse. She was so mad she flung the filmy thing right in my face. "Here, take it," she yelled. "It's ruined now anyway!" Then she grabbed her coat and went slamming out the door.

Standing with the blouse draped over my head, I felt awful. But I thought I might as well make the best of it, so I went upstairs and put it away in my drawer.

Hidden at the back of the drawer, underneath my underwear, was a printed rejection slip from *Love Story* magazine. Secretly I had written a fabulous story about a handsome hero named Lance who had hung himself in his bedroom closet when he was jilted by his lady-love. But the hook broke and he ended up with only a sore neck. When Angela, his paramour, found out what he had done she was so remorseful that she married him. But they didn't live happily ever after because they found out that they didn't really like each other, never mind love, so they got a divorce.

Seeing that rejection slip was the last straw. I decided I *had* to see my Aunt Milly. All my life when I had serious problems I took them to Aunt Milly. Mum said her little sister attracted troubles like honey draws flies.

Aunt Milly was fifteen years younger than Mum and fifteen years older than me. So she was still young enough to remember what it was like to be fifteen. And she still looked like a girl. She had long auburn ringlets, bright sparrow's eyes and blood-red fingernails. She wore spike heels and short skirts and she still had a girlish figure in spite of the fact that she'd had three children one right after the other. Lots of people criticized Aunt Milly and said she should grow up and act her age. But Mum said jealousy would get them nowhere.

Aunt Milly and Uncle Mort lived in a house just like ours on Durie Street. So on Monday I stopped in after school.

"Halloo, Bea!" The door swung open as wide as her smile. "You're just in time to share a Coca Cola."

A bucket of soapy water with a string mop sticking out of it was sitting in a puddle on the kitchen floor. "Oh, I'm sorry if I'm interrupting your spring cleaning, Aunt Milly," I apologized. Mum had our house turned upside down with spring cleaning, and I knew she wouldn't thank anybody for dropping in unannounced.

"Oh, bother spring cleaning," snorted my carefree auntie. "I don't go by seasons. If it's dirty I clean it, whether it needs it or not."

We laughed and joked as she put sweater-coats on Bonny and Dimples, her two little girls, and chased them out to play. Then she gave Sunny, her boy, a quarter and sent him up to the Cut-rate Meat-market on Bloor Street for a pound of sausages for supper.

When we were alone, she tiptoed across the clean half of the floor in her spike heels (she never wore house shoes, even when she was cleaning) and lifted the top of the icebox. "I just got fifty pounds of ice an hour ago, so this pop should be good and cold. But if Morty forgets to empty the ice pan one more time I'm going to order up a Frigidaire."

"You sound just like Mum," I laughed as she snapped the cap off the frosty green bottle and handed it to me for the first sip. "Every night at bedtime she says, 'Did you empty the ice pan, Jim?' and Dad answers, 'Always do.' Then Mum grumbles, 'Well, you always don't because there was a puddle on my clean waxed linoleum this morning.'"

Aunt Milly chuckled, then she said seriously, "Fran works too hard. It'll be the death of her." Sitting down at the table, she kicked off her shoes, put her feet up on a chair and said, "A penny for your thoughts, Bea?" She could always tell.

So I began to pour my heart out. I told her all about how Mum and Dad were still mad at me for smoking, and how Lorne had gone back to Gloria Carlyle after Dad pushed him down our porch steps, and how Willa had discover the dirt on her peach blouse and wasn't speaking to me, and how I couldn't find a job to save my life, and how *Love Story* magazine had rejected my romance. "Now Georgie Dunn is all crazy about dopey Wanda Backhouse again, so I haven't got a boyfriend, and I haven't got any decent clothes, and I know I'll never be a writer. And besides, I don't think I'm going to pass this year."

Aunt Milly took another sip of Coke and shoved the bottle across the table to me. "I've got an idea about a job at least," she said, her dark eyes twinkling conspiratorially. "I'm going to be working at your Aunt Susan's store for the summer. How would you like to work there with me?"

"Oh, Aunt Milly, do you think I could? I've never used a cash register and I might cheat somebody."

"Just so long as it's not your Aunt Susan!" she laughed. "Anyhoo . . . keep it under your hat until I get a chance to talk to Susan. She generally likes her helpers to be older than you because she says the young ones eat up all her profits. But I think I can get around her in your case."

I knew if anybody could get around her, Aunt Milly could. She had a reputation for being able to wrap all sorts of people around her little finger. And she was Aunt Susan's favourite sister. Everybody knew that.

"Now for your part of the bargain, Bea. You'll have to set your mind to passing your exams so you'll be free for the summer. And stop worrying about boys. Boys are like streetcars — there's always another one coming along. Just you remember, young lady, you've got a little bit of 'it' and you got it from your Aunt Milly." I loved to hear her say that. It made my heart feel five pounds lighter.

"And about that story of yours," continued my optimistic aunt, "well, you probably sent it to the wrong magazine. Love stories are supposed to have happy endings. It sounds more like a *True Story* to me." Of course! Why hadn't I thought of that?

Just then Sunny came back with the sausages and Aunt Milly sent him out to the backyard to amuse Bonny and Dimples while she finished up the floor.

"I have to run, Aunt Milly," I said, startled to see that it was five o'clock by the clock on top of the kitchen cabinet. "Mum's gone downtown and I have to make supper."

My hand was on the front doorknob when Aunt Milly said, "Just a tick." She dashed upstairs and down again with a pink sweater in her hand. "Try this on for size," she said with that wonderful twinkle in her eye.

"Oh, Aunt Milly, it looks brand new!" I pulled it on and did up the pearl buttons. It fit like a glove.

"Like it?"

"Do I!"

"Then it's yours."

"But — but — it's your new sweater."

"Well, fiddle-de-dee! When you give something away you always get back double."

That was her philosophy. Mum said her little sister was the living end. She'd give you the shirt right off her back — literally.

"Toodle-oo! Love you!" she called from her front stoop. I turned on the run and blew her a kiss.

That very night I practically begged Arthur to help me with my homework. He looked at me skeptically, but grudgingly agreed, and from then on he helped me every night, with some prodding from Mum and Dad. They were both pleased as punch with my sudden interest in school, so they weren't mad at me anymore. And I passed my exams.

Sure as her word, Aunt Milly wrapped Aunt Susan around her little finger and got me my first summer job, at the Uptown Nuthouse.

11
The Nuthouse

I was tickled pink, as well as dressed in pink, as I hurried up the street on the first day of my new job. Lost in thought, daydreaming about the new clothes I would buy — real silk stockings, step-ins instead of bloomers, and maybe even spectator pumps — I hardly noticed Roy-Roy sitting on the porch in his rocking chair, his head lolling down on his chest.

Usually I stopped to talk to him no matter what. But on this particular day I would have just passed by if he hadn't called out "Ba-Ba! Ba-Ba!" I knew that meant "Bea-Bea! Bea-Bea!"

I crossed the road and hurried up the walk. "Hi, Roy-Roy," I said. "I'm sorry I can't stop to visit with you today. I'm on my way to work and I haven't got time."

Poor Roy-Roy, he tried so hard to communicate. He rolled his head and flailed his arms and slobber flew in big drops from his gaping mouth. I reached out and touched his bony shoulder — he had gotten so thin lately. "I'm sorry, Roy-Roy. I'll come back another time, okay? Bye for now."

"Ba-ba-ba!" he cried pitifully after me. I turned around to wave to him, but his head was already slumped down on his chest again.

It was an hour's ride on the Bloor streetcar from Durie Street to Yonge and I'd been given strict orders to be there at ten o'clock sharp. I managed to dash breathlessly in the door at ten minutes after ten.

"Well, Lady Jane!" Aunt Susan came scurrying from the back of the store with a load of raw cashew butts. "Better late than never, I always say."

"I'm sorry, Aunt Susan. I missed a streetcar because I stopped to talk to Roy-Roy."

"Never you mind, Bea" — she gave me a welcoming smile — "I'm just pulling your leg. Where's your funnybone?"

Relieved, I went behind the counter, took off my new sweater, folded it carefully and put it on a high shelf where it wouldn't get dirty.

"Where's Aunt Milly?" I asked anxiously.

"She'll be here any minute. She phoned to say she'd be late because Gertie Witherspoon, that good-for-nothing layabout who minds her children, hadn't got there yet. Milly pays her fifty cents a day too. It's highway robbery if you ask me."

"What should I do?" I asked hesitantly. I'd heard that Aunt Susan was a tartar to work for, so I was nervous as a cat being alone with her.

"Just make boxes until the noon-hour rush." She handed me a pile of flat, odd-shaped pieces of cardboard. I tried every which way to bend and twist those darn things into boxes, but all I succeeded in doing was tearing the end flaps off.

"Good gravy, Bea, if you keep that up you'll owe

me money before the day's out. Here now, pay attention."

Deftly, with practised fingers, she creased and shaped those boxes, tucking the end flaps in and snapping the lids shut so you could see the picture of the squirrel on the top with the acorn in its paws. Under him, in red letters, were the words *The Uptown Nuthouse,* and along the sides it read *Nuts to you!*

But even after being shown, I had trouble. It reminded me of the time I tried to teach Billy how to tie his shoestrings. It looked so easy when you knew how.

Just then Aunt Milly came breezing in the door with a cheery "Halloo!" and my heart sang at the sight of her. In seconds she taught me the trick of folding the boxes, and in minutes I was an expert box-maker.

At noon the store quickly filled with customers. It was a nice day and the door stood wide open. The lovely smell of roasting cashews went drifting down the street, tempting everybody within half a mile.

Aunt Milly taught me how to weigh the nuts and figure out the price on a little pad.

"I'm not good at arithmetic," I apologized nervously.

"By the end of the day you will be." She gave me a good-natured poke in the ribs. "But don't expect to learn everything at once. Just leave the money on the till and I'll ring it in. Now, it's up to us to wait on customers while Susan does the cooking, so look a-lackey!" Mum often said that and I knew it meant "Look alive!" So I did.

The gas cooker was in the front window of the shop where it could be seen from the street. All day long people pressed their noses against the steamy glass to watch Aunt Susan stir the nuts in the big iron cauldron. And all day long they streamed through the open door, with a string of crazy, nutsy jokes about how things were in the "Nuthouse." It was more fun than a picnic.

Aunt Milly knew practically everybody by name. "And how's my Ernie today?" she inquired of the shoeshine boy as she gave him ten cents worth of peanuts for a nickel. "What's your pleasure, Curley?" she asked the Eaton's driver who had parked beside a no-parking sign to dash into the store. "How's the old ticker, Meggie?" She showed genuine concern for the pale-faced woman who tottered in on shaky legs.

That first day I met almost all the regular customers, from the blind man who ran the newspaper stall at the corner of Yonge and Bloor to John David Eaton himself.

"Here comes Mr. Eaton!" Aunt Susan announced, all a-twitter as she wiped her greasy hands on her greasy apron. "I'll look after him myself."

I couldn't help but stare at the man who owned the giant department store where all Toronto did its shopping. He looked right at me and smiled, so I smiled back, just as if he was an ordinary man. I couldn't get over it.

"Wait'll I tell Mum!" I whispered to Aunt Milly. She was nibbling hazelnuts behind the cash register. I followed suit and popped a handful into my mouth.

When the great man had left, Aunt Susan declared, "He's a fine, well-to-do gentleman, is Mr. Eaton." She was proud as a peacock of her most illustrious customer. "He took two five-pound boxes of my best mixture," she boasted.

"Well, he might be fine and he might be as rich as Rockefeller," snapped Aunt Milly, punching the cash register keys noisily, "but he's not one wit better than the rest of us mortals. The cat can look at the queen, you know!" I wasn't sure what the connection was, but I got the message anyway.

That was a big day for celebrities. About an hour later, who should come in but Mister Gordon Sinclair, the *Star*'s famous newspaperman. I recognized him from his picture and my eyes nearly popped out of my head. Aunt Susan and Mr. Sinclair had a running joke going about which one of them was going to become a millionaire first. Aunt Susan got a great kick out of that.

Later still, when business had slowed down (actually, there was hardly ever a minute when the store was empty) a tired-looking young woman came in. Her coat was shabby and threadbare and she was carrying a baby in a faded blue blanket. Two little hollow-cheeked girls clung to her skirts.

"Five cents worth of redskins, please," she said in a quiet voice. She held out a nickel in her chapped red hand.

As I began to scoop the hot, fresh nuts onto the scales, I glanced quickly at Aunt Susan. Her back was to me and she was humming "The Old Grey Mare" as she cooked in the window. I could hear Aunt Milly rattling tins in the storeroom. Nobody else was in sight. So, quicker than you could say "Jack Robinson" I loaded up a five-pound bag and handed it over the counter. I took the nickel, my heart thudding.

The young mother's eyes filled with tears. Stuffing the oily brown sack under the baby's frayed blanket, she turned and scurried out the door without a backward glance, the little girls scampering after her.

"What a mess that one was!" Aunt Susan glanced up with the dripping wooden spoon in her hand. "Did she buy anything?"

"Sure!" I sighed with relief. "A nickel's worth of peanuts."

"Well, last of the big-time spenders!" snorted Aunt Susan. If she knew the truth she'd fire me on the spot.

After a long day during which we had no time to eat anything except nuts, Aunt Milly and I climbed wearily onto a westbound Bloor streetcar. I was carrying a big box of mixed nuts home to Mum (the second best mixture) but I wasn't the least bit tempted to dip into them. For once in my life I'd had my fill.

"How much did Susan pay you, Bea?" asked Aunt Milly.

"Two dollars," I said, "and carfare."

"Well, she must think you're the cat's meow because that's exactly what she pays me." She didn't say it jealously, she said it joyously. "See? Didn't I tell you every cloud has a silver lining?"

"Speaking of silver, Aunt Milly —" I knew I had to confess to somebody and she was the ideal person, so I told her about the woman with the three children that I'd given a huge bag of redskins to for a nickel. "She looked so poor and hungry," I explained.

Well, you could have knocked me over with a feather when my loving, generous aunt frowned and said, "It's all right this time, Bea. But don't let it happen again. I know why you did it. The same reason I gave the shoeshine boy a little extra. Poor little nipper — his old man drinks up every cent he brings home. But you have to be careful not to get taken in. Some people dress like ragbags to fool the likes of you and me. And half the time they could buy and sell the both of us. And make no mistake, Bea, your Aunt Susan deserves every cent she gets. She's worked her fingers to the bone building up her business, right through the Depression, with no help from anybody. Don't you forget that."

I promised I wouldn't. I was really surprised to learn that there actually were people in the world who would pull a mean trick like that. But I was absolutely sure the young mother, who had been too choked up to say thank you, wasn't one of them. So I didn't really feel guilty. Just glad I didn't get caught.

That night I recorded everything that had happened in my diary. When I read it over, I thought to myself, "This would make a swell story . . . if *only* I could be a writer."

12

Long time no see!

Summer was nearly over when I got a letter from Aunt Aggie. She was Dad's sister who lived in Muskoka, in the log house she was born in. Long ago the little house had been crowded with people — parents and grandparents and children — but now Aunt Aggie was all alone.

Heckley, Muskoka,
August 21, 1938

Dear Niece,
  Long time no see! (Where did Aunt Aggie learn those modern slang sayings, I wondered, isolated up there in the wilderness?) *Lovely sunshiny day today. Not too hot. For some reason you've been on my mind all day, so I decided it was high time I sent you a line. I haven't heard a peep out of you since your Grandpa Thomson passed on. It's lonely here in the log house without him, even if he was an old curmudgeon. Ouch! I bit my tongue on a bit of sprucegum. Serves me right for speaking ill of the dead.*
  Got a letter from your father last Saturday. He says you are a working girl now making big money in

your aunt's nut shop. Just thinking about those scrumptious nuts makes my mouth water. She gave me a pound once and I doled them out to myself and made them last two months. Haven't tasted the likes of them since.

I don't suppose you'd have time to slide up for a visit before school starts? I've sure missed you these past few summers. Every time I cross the creek coming home from the post office I remember the bloodsuckers stuck to your leg and I can't help laughing. Imagine you thinking you'd be sucked to death. Poor little thing.

Yesterday I stopped in on Lily Huxtable. She gave me tea. Horace and Daisy both asked for you. (Horace and Daisy Huxtable were my best friends in Heckley.) *I had to say I hadn't heard from you in a dog's age. How about dropping your old aunt a line? And tell that brother of mine if he'll send you up by train I'll see you get back. You can hitch a ride in from Huntsville with Jimmy Hobbs — he's Hannibal's baby brother, in case you forgot. Jimmy meets the train from the big smoke* (that's what Aunt Aggie called Toronto) *every afternoon. He's our mailman now. Good steady job for a young fella. He'll make a good catch for some lucky girl in a few years' time.*

I cut oats this morning, then gathered a honey pail of big, juicy huckleberries this afternoon. Got lots of cream — you could eat your fill! One of my chickens got killed last night and the pig ate it. Don't that beat all? Well, if you come up we'll eat the pig just for spite. Ha, ha!

Have to turn in now. Must clean this lamp chim-

*ney tomorrow. I can hardly see what I'm writing, so
excuse the hen scratches. It's eleven p.m. Write soon.*

Lovingly,
your Aunt Aggie.

I showed the letter to Mum. She stopped ironing
to read it. "I think it's a good idea for you to visit your
Aunt Aggie, Bea." She folded the dishtowels on the
board stretched between two chair backs. Mum was
an incurable ironer. She even ironed dust rags!

"I'd love to go, Mum, but what would Aunt Susan
say? I don't want to lose my job. It's the best job I ever
had."

"I know, Booky, but you're getting piqued looking. And I think you've lost some weight. You know
what they say — a change is as good as a rest.
Besides, you'll have to give it up when school starts,
so one week won't make much difference."

"Will you ask Aunt Susan for me then?"

"I'll get Milly to ask her."

So once again Aunt Milly wrapped Aunt Susan
around her little finger and off I went to Muskoka.

Sure enough, Jimmy Hobbs was there to meet
me in Huntsville. He was kind of cute and we took a
shine to each other right off the bat. We flirted all the
way to Heckley in the mail truck. After dropping off
the mail sack, he drove me right to the log-house
door.

Aunt Aggie was outside looking expectantly up
the road. I jumped out and we squealed and hugged
each other. Holding me at arm's length, she declared,
"You're a sight for sore eyes, Bea!"

"So are you!" I cried.

She hadn't changed a bit. Her straw-coloured hair was still piled up like a cowflap on top of her head, her skin was brown and lined from the sun, and her wire spectacles were perched on the end of her nose. And, if I wasn't mistaken, she was still wearing the same calico housedress and low-heeled house shoes, and the black cotton stockings that wrinkled around her ankles.

But she couldn't get over the change in me. "Why, you're all grown up, Bea. Your grandpa — may he rest in peace — would hardly know you. Where on earth did that little scatterbrain go who used to take her bath in a tub of rainwater beside the house?"

"The same place as the kid who used to braid bracelets out of Major's tail." I laughed excitedly. "By the way, how is Major?"

"Oh, he'll do for an old fella."

"I'll go see him after supper," I said.

"Well, come in and stay awhile. You must be starved." Suddenly we both remembered Jimmy Hobbs. He was swinging on the truck door, grinning awkwardly. "Would you care to join us for a bite, Jimmy?" invited Aunt Aggie.

"No, thanks just as much, Miss Thomson." Aunt Aggie and I were both Miss Thomsons since she'd never married. "I'll be going now. But if you've no objection, I'll drop around tomorrow."

He tried not to look at me as he said this, but we both managed to slide our eyes towards each other without moving our heads. Aunt Aggie didn't miss a thing.

"Sure, Jimmy, anytime. You're always welcome."

He drove off with a wave and we went inside the log house. It seemed like ages since I'd been there. When Grandpa Thomson died, just Dad and Aunt Ida and Uncle Charlie had come up for the funeral. Dad and Uncle Charlie had dug their father's grave themselves.

A fire crackled in the wood stove, but it was a cool day so the room wasn't too warm.

Gradually my eyes adjusted to the house's dim interior. Great-Grandpa Thomson, one of the first settlers in Heckley, had built the log house in 1848 — you could still read the date carved over the low doorway. Two narrow kitchen windows were on either side of the big black range. A yellow fly-sticker hung over the wood box. Dozens of flies were stuck on it, some still alive, buzzing frantically. Mum never used fly-stickers because she said they were too unsightly. Instead she set poison pads in saucers of water on the window sills. The unsuspecting flies would come for a drink, take one sip and drop dead.

As if reading my mind, Aunt Aggie said, "It's time I put up a new one of them eyesores." Taking the loaded sticker down, she dropped it into the hot stove. It flared and sizzled and cremated all the flies. Then she unrolled a nice new one and thumbtacked it to the same ceiling beam. In seconds two flies were trapped, their feet stuck fast, their wings fluttering in a wild frenzy.

"Muskoka is a fierce place for flies and skeeters," remarked Aunt Aggie. "It's all the lakes and ponds that breed the filthy vermin. Ah, well," she shrugged resignedly, "I guess we need the little beggars to remind us we're alive."

I laughed at her homey joke as I gazed around the old familiar room, at the homemade wooden furniture on the bare plank floors, and the old-fashioned pictures on the rough pine walls. The only thing that was different was the 1938 calendar tacked to the back of the door leading to the woodshed. On it was a picture of the Dionne quintuplets looking like five little pink dolls. I noticed the day of my arrival was circled in red and Aunt Aggie had written inside the circle, *Bea's coming!* That sure made me feel good.

Aunt Aggie already had the table laid with Great-Grandma Thomson's china tea set, brought all the way from Nottingham in 1847. Two bowls of big, sugar-frosted huckleberries sat on the hand-embroidered tablecloth. She wrapped a flannel cloth around her right hand and lifted a pan of steaming baking-powder biscuits out of the hot oven. Then we sat down cosily together.

13
Story time

Over the table Grandpa Thomson frowned down on us from his homemade criss-crossed frame. There used to be a baby's picture in that frame, I remembered. I think it was Dad's little brother, who died of the ague. But I guess Aunt Aggie had replaced it with her father's picture so she wouldn't be so lonely. His eyes seemed to be watching every bite we ate. He sure would have been upset at all the butter we were slathering on our biscuits.

Aunt Aggie read my mind. "What he don't know can't hurt us now, Bea. He was a stingy old codger and there's no denying it. But I miss him just the same and I hope he's resting easy beside Ma." Her plain face clouded over. She rubbed her eyes underneath her glasses. "They had a hard row to hoe here in the wilderness. You come from hardy stock, Bea, and that's a fact."

It was the first time I'd given much thought to my roots. On both sides of my family I sprang from pioneers. And in a sense Aunt Aggie was still a pioneer. She hauled her water from the spring, cut her own firewood and stacked it up for winter, filled her pantry with wild preserves and buried her vegetables in the root cellar. She cleaned oil lamps and milked the cow and churned the butter and went deer hunting in season. She was a good shot too.

"Last winter I bagged a buck that was so big he fed every soul in Heckley for two months," she bragged.

"How come it didn't spoil without an ice box?"

"Hung it out in the woodshed." She inclined her head towards the woodshed door. "It's cold as charity out there in wintertime. Go look in the parlour and you'll see his head. Antlers six feet wide. Stuffed him myself, I did."

I poked my head into the musty, unused parlour. Sure enough, a huge head stared at me from gaping, empty sockets. "Where's his eyes?" I shut the door with a shudder.

"Oh, I never got around to ordering glass ones from Elwood Peebles, the taxidermist in Huntsville. You can't leave the real eyes in, you know. They'd go all maggoty."

"Oh, Aunt Aggie!" Suddenly her existence seemed primitive, almost barbaric. "Why don't you sell this old place and come to live with us or Uncle Charlie?"

"Live in the city?" You'd think I'd suggested she go live in a jungle. "Well, if it ever comes to that you'd better order me up a plot in the nearest graveyard because I'd be dead in a month. All that noise and confusion, folks rushing every which way like ants on a sandhill, smoke and fumes from motor cars, and so many electric lights you can't even find the Big Dipper at night. And what in tarnation would I do to keep body and soul together? I got no skills to speak of. Up here I get along just dandy. I can barter and trade with my neighbours for anything I need. I bake bread for Lily and she knits stockings for me. Barney Usher does my ploughing in spring and I help with his haying in summer. Around these parts we're like kinfolk. We look out for each other."

She filled both our cups with strong tea and put a dollop of cream on my third dish of huckleberries. "There's more to life in the country than meets the eye, Bea," she continued thoughtfully. "Why, only last week I was putting a bunch of daisies on Ma's grave — it was her birthday. It's twenty-two years since she passed away and I still miss her . . ."

"I know what you mean," I nodded wisely. "Grampa Cole has been gone for almost two years now, but it seems like only yesterday. I still say, 'Hi, Grampa!' when I pass his house, and I can almost hear him answering, 'Hallo, there, Be-*a*-trice, how's my girl?'"

"Then you understand how I feel. You'd have liked your grandma, Bea. We're alike as three peas in a pod, you and her and me. Well, as I was saying, I was setting a jar of yellow daisies out when I heard the sound of snapping twigs behind me. I scrunched around, expecting company, when lo and behold, I found myself staring eyeball to eyeball with a big black bear."

"Oh, Aunt Aggie! What did you do?"

"I just sat still on my haunches and stared him out. I could tell he wasn't crazed because he was calm and he wasn't frothing. In a few minutes he ambled off into the bush and went about his business. Now where on earth would you see a sight like that in the city, I ask you?"

I had to admit you'd never see a bear in Toronto, except in Riverdale Zoo. And then he'd be in a cage.

She told me a lot more hair-raising stories and exciting adventures. Then she asked about my job at the Nuthouse.

"Oh, that reminds me," I cried. "I brought you a present." I undid the clasp of my old leather grip and instantly the lovely aroma of fresh nuts escaped into the room. Aunt Aggie sniffed and wiggled her nose.

Handing her the big box with the squirrel on top, I announced proudly, "It's five pounds of our *best* mixture. And Aunt Susan sends her warmest regards too."

"That's mighty generous of her. Tell her I said thanks a bunch." She picked out a big cashew and placed it on her tongue. "Will you have one, Bea?" she offered.

"No, thanks. I'm sick of nuts. But I love working at the Nuthouse." Then I told her all about it. "Everybody comes there, Aunt Aggie. And some of the people are rich and famous. Aunt Milly said she even filled an order for the governor of New York State once. Imagine!"

"It sounds like a grand job," said Aunt Aggie, still savouring the same nut.

"It is. And Aunt Susan says I can work there for the Christmas rush if I stop acting the fool with Red Macpherson. Red is a boy who comes in after school to help clean up. He's loads of fun. He swears like a trooper and throws peanuts in the shell at me to get my attention. Aunt Susan gets hopping mad and says she's going to take every peanut out of our pay. But she never does."

Chuckling with delight, Aunt Aggie piled the dishes in the graniteware dishpan, covered them with rainwater and set the pan on the stove to warm up. Then she sat down again. "Tell me more," she urged. "I haven't had such a good chinwag in a month of Sundays."

So I told her about the excitement we'd had a few days before I left home. "You should have been there," I announced. "Aunt Milly had just rung up a big sale when a man yelled, 'Gimme all your money.'"

"Mercy," said Aunt Aggie. "What did she do?"

"She gave him all that was in the till, but Aunt Susan had just cleaned it out, so he didn't get much. Then he yelled at everybody to get out of his way and nobody would get hurt, so they all squeezed up and made a path for him and he escaped. *Then* guess what Aunt Susan did?"

"Heaven only knows!"

"She took after him with the wooden paddle she stirs the nuts with, hollering 'Stop! Thief! Police!'"

"Did he get away?"

"No, because Big Bill Brown, the Yonge Street policeman was going by and stuck out his foot just in time to trip him and send him sprawling. When Aunt Susan got there she started beating the thief with her paddle. She got all her money back too — seventy-five dollars."

"Your Aunt Susan's mighty foolhardy. Did the man have a gun?"

"Yeah, only it was carved out of soap and covered with shoe black."

"You may have a grand job, Bea" said Aunt Aggie, "but it sounds like a dangerous one."

"Not for me," I pointed out. "Aunt Milly's the cashier. You should have heard Aunt Susan bawling her out for giving away her hard-earned money. Aunt Milly got mad and started to leave, but Aunt Susan apologized and everything got back to normal."

I went on talking all the time the water heated and Aunt Aggie did up the dishes. She wouldn't let me help. By then the big lamp was lit and the old log house was filled with mysterious shadows. Finally she said, "I could listen all night, but you must be plumb tuckered from your trip and I have to get up with the chickens."

So she lit us each a candle and blew out the oil lamp. Then she unlatched the stairwell door and led the way up the ancient, creaky stairs.

I thought I'd be bored stiff in Muskoka for a whole week. But the time whizzed by so fast it made my head spin. Aunt Aggie was swell company. And one night Jimmy Hobbs took me to a picture show at the Town Hall in nearby Elmsdale. We went in the mail truck. He said it was against government regulations but he didn't care. It was a silent picture starring Laurel and Hardy, which reminded me of my childhood. All the pictures in Toronto were talkies now.

Afterwards we went to a soda fountain and Jimmy ordered a whole brick of ice cream cut in half and served on two glass plates. Then he ordered a bottle of Whistle and two straws and we shared it with our heads together.

Another time Daisy and Horace Huxtable and Jimmy and I went to a church social in Heckley. That was the first time two boys ever fought to sit beside me. It was thrilling except that it hurt Daisy's feelings and I didn't like that. After supper there was square-dancing and I was surprised at how fast I learned the steps. Of course, Jimmy was a good teacher.

I was sorry when it was time to go home. Jimmy drove me to the train and kissed me goodbye — twice. We promised faithfully to write to each other.

Relaxing in the soft red seat on the way home I had time to think. I realized now that Aunt Aggie's life in the wilderness was full to overflowing with zest and excitement and wealth — not money, but another kind of wealth, the kind money can't buy.

And Mum had been right about a change being as good as a rest. I felt marvellous!

Aunt Milly had been right too. Boys were just like streetcars — there was always another one coming along.

14
Sad news

I was surprised to see Dad waiting for me at the West Toronto station. I hadn't expected anyone to meet me. He must have just finished his ten-hour work shift because he was carrying his lunch pail. I noticed he looked tired and a bit old. It was funny, I thought, how people seemed to change when you didn't see them for a while. Even as short a time as a week.

As soon as we were settled on the streetcar I started telling him what a good time I'd had and how much I admired his sister. He nodded, looking away from me out the window. It was then I realized that something was wrong. I felt a swift stab of fear. "What's the matter, Dad?" Suddenly I remembered Mum going around holding her heart. "Is it Mum? Is she sick?"

"No, Bea. No." He gave my hand a reassuring pat. "It's not family. But your mother thought I'd better tell you on the way home before you hear it on the street, since you were so fond of him."

"Who?"

"Well — it's young Roy-Roy."

"What about Roy-Roy?"

"He passed away yesterday, Bea."

I was so shocked I couldn't speak. I felt numb all over.

Passed away. That's what Aunt Aggie had said about Grandma and Grandpa. They'd passed away. What a strange word to use for dying. You "pass" people on the street. You "pass" an exam at school. You "pass" in a card game. But where on earth do you "pass away" to? I wondered.

"You mean he died," I said bluntly.

"Yes. He died."

Walking silently down Veeny Street, we "passed" Roy-Roy's house. There was the rocking chair he had been sitting on the day I was in too much of a hurry to visit. He had spent the last year of his life in that rickety old rocker, swaying to and fro, thinking things nobody knew. Suddenly I noticed something strange. "There's no wreath on the door," I said.

"No. He's at the Undertaking Parlour. Rachel's too broke up to have him at home."

"Won't that cost a lot of money?" I had heard that it cost as much as two hundred dollars. That's why everybody we knew got buried from home.

"It seems like Rachel's got more money than anybody surmised," Dad said. "I hear tell she's paid cash for the funeral, and the young lad's laid out in a solid oak coffin."

That brought to mind what Aunt Milly had said. "Some people dress like ragbags to fool the likes of you and me, and they could buy and sell the both of us." It's amazing how she knew things like that.

The funeral was to be held the next day. Our gang on Veeny Street had gone together and sent a huge basket of flowers. I was glad when Mum told me they had remembered to put my name on the card.

We decided to go in a group to the funeral, so we met in Aunt Ellie's kitchen. Six of the boys — Georgie, Arthur, Buster, Charlie, Alvin and Elmer — had been asked to be pallbearers.

The minute we entered the Undertaking Parlour my legs turned to jelly. Glad grabbed my elbow. She always knew when I was in danger of keeling over. I had never set foot in a funeral parlour before in my whole life. It seemed sinister and mysterious, filled with hushed voices and muffled music and the heavy scent of flowers.

A man in a black suit and dough-coloured skin met us in the front foyer. "Whom do you wish to view?" he asked in a funereal tone. View! Cold fingers traced up my spine.

"Roy-Roy the dumb . . ." Georgie stopped, embarrassed.

"Roy Butterbaugh," explained Arthur, unconsciously copying the man's weird monotone.

The undertaker pointed a pale finger. "Mr. Butterbaugh is resting in the chapel straight ahead," he said.

Mister! Resting! Roy-Roy!

We crept in a cluster down the long corridor, the sound of our footsteps smothered in the thick maroon carpet. Plush furniture and gloomy pictures lined the dark-papered walls.

The sign over the chapel archway read: *Mr. Randolph Roy Butterbaugh.* We exchanged incredulous glances.

"Randolph! What a beautiful name," whispered Ada in a soft, surprised voice.

The miniature church was overflowing with blossoms. The fragrance was almost overpowering. "I think I'm going to be sick!" gasped Ruth, pressing her hanky to her mouth.

Slowly we made our way down the aisle between the polished pews. Then we all gathered around the shiny wooden casket.

Roy-Roy looked incredibly handsome. He was all dressed up in a dark suit with a blue tie and white shirt. Now he didn't need a bib to catch the slobber from his lips. Now his fine-boned hands didn't flail uselessly in the air. His usually tousled brown hair was combed in neat waves back from his white brow. His features were smooth, no longer twisted with the terrible effort to speak.

"I didn't realize how handsome he was," Ruth whispered.

We all murmured in agreement.

"He was the most beautiful baby the Lord ever made." Rachel came out from a curtained-off alcove and stood beside us. She wore a plain black dress (just one), and her normally dishevelled hair was pulled back in a smooth brown bun. She barely resembled the Raggie Rachel we all knew.

We stepped back respectfully as she approached the coffin. Leaning down towards her son, she whispered, "Sweet dreams, little one," the way a mother would whisper to her sleeping baby.

Then she sat in the front pew and patted the space beside her. "Sit here, Be-*a*-trice," she said. I was surprised. Only one other person had ever pronounced my name that way, my Grampa Cole. She motioned to the rest of our gang. "All of you sit around me. You were Roy's family," she told us. "You were his brothers and sisters."

The chapel was full when the service began.

During the eulogy Rachel's eyes never left Roy-Roy's sweet face. She had insisted that the coffin be left open, as if to keep him with her as long as possible.

"*Auf Wiedersehen,* my dear," I heard her murmur.

I thought I'd choke to death on the lump in my throat. Everyone was crying all over the chapel. I wept openly, full of regret and sorrow, wishing with all my heart that I had given my sick "brother" more of my time. Why, oh, why hadn't I stopped longer that day on the way to work?

After the service our whole gang rode with Rachel in the long black limousine to Park Lawn Cemetery. Only a stone's throw away was Grampa Cole's grave. I couldn't even look in that direction.

A canvas canopy fluttered over the open grave site. As the clergyman said "Ashes to ashes . . ." the oak casket was slowly lowered into the ground. The last thing I saw, through a blur of tears, was Rachel's huge spray of flowers tied with a wide blue ribbon. On the ribbon, in gold letters, were the words *My Beloved Son*. The pain in my throat was excruciating.

Afterwards, instead of going back to the deceased person's house, which was the custom, Rachel did the most extraordinary thing — eccentric, the grown-ups called it. Totally ignoring them, she gathered our gang around her and invited us all to Hunt's Bakery on Bloor Street. And we rode there in the long black limousine!

At the back of the bakery, entirely separate from the bake shop, was an ice-cream parlour. "Sit yourselves down." She waved us to the white enamelled tables. "I've ordered treats all round."

"I won't be able to swallow a mouthful," I whispered to Glad.

"Me neither," she answered huskily.

But when the chocolate eclairs and ice-cream sodas were set before us our appetites miraculously returned. Rachel sat alone at a table by the wall drinking cup after cup of black tea. She watched us with a sad smile through dark-circled, glistening eyes.

The very next day she moved away and didn't take a thing with her. Neighbours said she just walked up the street and was gone. Weeks passed, and when she didn't return, workmen were sent in to clean out her cottage. "They had to use shovels," Mum said, clucking her tongue. "There wasn't a blessed thing worth salvaging."

One nice autumn evening a few weeks later Glad and I took a shortcut home from Sunnyside over the hill called the Camel's Back. As we passed the village dump, which was within sight (and smell) of our houses, we saw something red fluttering in the garbage heap. Holding our noses, we edged closer. The red thing was the remains of one of Rachel's raggedy dresses. And only a few feet away, almost buried under the trash, were the broken pieces of Roy-Roy's old rocking chair.

We broke into a run, the tears coursing down our cheeks.

15

The bravest man I know

After Roy-Roy died, life sank into the doldrums.

Then one day when Winn was reading the pink Tely she said, "Here's something right up your alley, Bea."

"What? Let me see!" I made a grab for the paper but missed.

"Just keep your shirt on," she teased. "I might be interested myself."

I made another grab and managed to snatch it out of her hand. Scanning the first page, all I could see was bad news about the war clouds gathering over Europe. Mum and Dad argued almost continually about that subject. Mum was sure another war was brewing, but Dad stubbornly insisted that the Great War, the one he'd fought in, had been the war to end all wars. "Besides," he declared to support his argument, "Mr. Chamberlain and Adolf Hitler have just signed a peace pact."

"Hmph!" Mum snorted. "It's probably not worth the paper it's written on." Sometimes they would wrangle like that for hours.

"For Pete's sake, Bea, open your peepers." Winn jabbed a broken fingernail at a paragraph near the bottom of the page that read:

Do you know a real live hero? Do you have a true story of valour to relate? If so, send it to our Story Editor in care of the Toronto Telegram, Bay and Melinda Streets. Your essay must not exceed two thousand words and must begin with the sentence: "The bravest man I know . . ." The rest is up to you. First prize is a genuine 14-karat gold Bulova (Bulova!) wristwatch, men's or ladies', valued by the T. Eaton Co. at $40.00 retail. Second prize is a crisp new ten-dollar bill, and five one-dollar bills will be awarded as consolation prizes. The decision of the judges is final. Good luck!

"Gee, thanks, Winn. I might have missed my chance."

I got the writing tablet and a pencil stub from a sideboard drawer and asked Dad to sharpen it with his penknife. I had decided to compose my story in pencil and recopy it in ink.

"Don't start that until the dishes are done," Mum said to me.

"I'll do them later," I promised. "Unless someone else will do them for me," I suggested hopefully.

Willa turned on me, disgusted. "Why don't you grow up? You've been saying that since you were ten years old. You're almost sixteen now and you're just as irresponsible as ever."

"She is not," objected Billy. He was always on my side.

"She is so," piped up Jakey. He always took the side opposite to Billy.

"You go ahead, Bea," Winn said obligingly. "I'll take your turn at the sink tonight since it was all my idea."

"She gets away with murder!" muttered a disgruntled Arthur.

"You should talk," I snapped back. "Stupid boys never do anything."

"Oh, ya? Who do you think invented the telephone?"

"Not you, that's for sure."

"Probably *Mrs.* Bell," Willa said dryly.

"The next one that says a word goes to bed," growled Dad.

Winn leaned in from the kitchen and made a zipping motion on her lips with soapy fingers. We all grinned. Then Dad went into the front room and snapped on the radio. He'd been awfully surly lately, so we all shut up and went about our business.

Sitting across the dining room table from Arthur, I was soon lost in thought. "The bravest man I know . . ." Grampa Cole was the first person to come to mind. He had saved countless lives from the Grenadier Pond without a thought for his own skin. But he was dead now, and the beginning sentence was definitely present tense.

I knew Dad had been a brave soldier during the Great War. He had a medal to prove it. But he hadn't done anything exactly heroic. Then there was Andy Beasley, the fireman who lived next door. He risked his life regularly and didn't even get paid for it because the Swansea Fire Department was manned by volunteers. Whenever the fire siren wailed at the top of Veeny Street we would hear Andy, through the thin wall that separated our houses, pounding down the stairs and out the door. It was very exciting and in summertime we'd all chase after him to see the fire. But still Andy wasn't my idea of a hero.

Suddenly, like a bolt out of the blue, I got an inspiration. My pencil began to fly across the page. Back and forth it went as if it travelled of its own accord.

When I was finished I copied the essay in ink, over and over again until I was convinced it was a flawless masterpiece of neatness and brilliance. I read it one last time and sighed with satisfaction.

Arthur glanced up. "Let's see it," he said.

"No!" I folded it quickly. "Read it in the paper."

"Fat chance!"

Ignoring his insult, I cut open a brown paper bag and made a big flat envelope. Slipping my precious manuscript inside, I glued it shut before anybody else could ask to see it. I addressed it in big block letters and Winn gave me stamps.

"Dad?" He had turned off the radio and was scowling at page one of the newspaper. I think he was afraid Mum might be right about the war. "What is it?" he asked.

"Will you post this on your way to work tomorrow?"

"Leave it under the sugar bowl," he said. Then he headed upstairs, saying he was all in.

That night, propped up on my pillow between Winn and Willa so I could breathe, I touched Winn's shoulder to see if she was still awake. If she wasn't, nothing short of a good wallop would disturb her. "Winn!" I whispered.

"Hmmm," came her drowsy reply.

"When I win the Bulova watch will you buy it off me for twenty dollars?"

"Don't you mean *if?*" put in Willa. I thought she was asleep.

"No, I mean when." I had never been so sure of anything in my whole life.

"It's a deal, kiddo," agreed Winn sleepily. Then she reached over her shoulder and gave me a limp handshake to seal the bargain.

The reason I needed the money more than the watch was because I'd already spent every cent I'd earned at Aunt Susan's store. I'd bought all my textbooks for third form, two new blouses, flesh-coloured celanese step-ins, a garter belt and three pairs of real silk stockings. Mum had bought me the saddle shoes I wanted, but I still needed a new fall coat.

With a self-satisfied sigh I finally fell asleep sitting up.

16
The winner!

Waiting for the day the winner would be announced seemed like an eternity. Then the miracle happened. There it was — my story! — on the second page of the pink Tely. Above it, a paragraph read:

Gold Watch Winner . . . The first prize of a genuine 14-karat gold Bulova watch, valued by the T. Eaton Company at $40.00, will be awarded to Miss Beatrice Myrtle Thomson of Swansea. Miss Thomson won for her unique and heartwarming story entitled: "The Bravest Man I Know Is a Woman." Congratulations, Miss Thomson, and best wishes for a successful writing career.

The story took up half the page. I was flushed and speechless (for once) with victory. Dad was flabbergasted that I had chosen his sister, Aunt Aggie, as my hero. Mum was proud as punch of me. "I hope L.M. Montgomery sees it," she cried, rubbing her hands together gleefully.

Mum had to go with me to the Telegram office to claim my prize because I was under age. I was the youngest contestant, they said. Mum couldn't get over that.

When we were outside on the street again, with the gold Bulova gleaming on my wrist, she said, "Let's celebrate, Booky. Just you and me."

So she took me to Loew's Theatre to see Nelson Eddy and Jeanette MacDonald in *Sweethearts,* and that was the end of Deanna Durbin. Oh, I still liked her a lot, but she wasn't my idol anymore. Now I had two idols, and the way they sang love songs to each other would tear your heart out by the roots.

Winn let me keep the watch for a while so I could show it off at school. Willa didn't say a word.

At school my popularity soared. Georgie and Lorne, who were both in fifth form now, started hanging around me as if I were a celebrity.

Sitting on the cafeteria bench eating lunch, Glad said, "Now you don't need to feel bad about your name not being on our Deanna Durbin picture. Winning a story contest is a lot more important anyway."

"I know," I agreed loftily. "Let's disband the Three Smart Girls Club. It seems so juvenile now."

"You're right, Bea," Ruth agreed. "At this stage in life we have more important things to do." Ruth had been extra busy lately practising for her piano recital at the Conservatory of Music.

At the far end of the table Gloria was sitting alone eating her fresh fruit salad. That's the kind of stuff she brought in her lunch every day. Imagine! "What's it like to be famous, Bea?" she called out, sort of sarcastically. She hadn't spoken to me for months.

"Marvellous! Simply marvellous!" I gloated.

"Oh, wow!" exlaimed Wanda. For once I thought her favourite word was suitable.

Mr. Ransom, our English teacher, read the story aloud to the class. He pointed out only two errors, which was pretty good for him.

For a whole week I basked in the warmth of my glory. I couldn't talk about anything else. Every time whoever I was with changed the subject I promptly changed it back again. Pretty soon I noticed that I was alone a lot. Glad was about the only friend I had left.

"I've decided to lengthen my story into a book and rename it 'Woman of the Wilderness,'" I confided in her one frosty fall day when the air was filled with the smell of burning leaves.

"Well, when you do, don't tell me about it," she snapped. "I can't stand any more of your bragging."

"Jealousy will get you nowhere," I snapped back as we parted and went in opposite directions.

But even Glad's turning traitor didn't dampen my spirits for long. Now that I was a person of letters, I decided I needed some new duds to spruce myself up. So that night I sold my watch to Winn for the twenty dollars she'd promised me.

On Saturday I went downtown by myself, since nobody would go with me, and bought the new fall coat I had my heart set on. It was pure wool, royal blue, with a wide leather belt. It cost $16.95. I had $3.05 left over, so I bought a hat to match, with a turned up brim. The saleslady put my old coat in the Eaton's box and I wore the new one home. I felt like a million in it.

Sauntering down Durie Street, I hoped I'd run into somebody I knew. I stopped at Aunt Milly's but she wasn't home. Disappointed, I looked around for someone, anyone, to show off to. Only the Canada Bread man came in sight. "Hi, Pete!" I waved at him gaily. When I was a little kid I used to holler at him every day, "Canada Bread is full of lead! The more you eat, the quicker you're dead!" But I'd outgrown that childishness long ago.

"You're looking mighty spiffy, Bea!" he called back above the clatter of old Barney's hooves.

As the bread wagon passed by I saw two little boys riding on the back step. Suddenly the kid in me jumped out and I yelled at the top of my lungs, "Hookey on behind!" The bread man didn't hear me but the boys did and they stuck their tongues out about a mile. That made me laugh all the way home. But I didn't meet another living soul. What a letdown.

When I stepped into the kitchen Mum stopped stirring the huge kettle of delicious-smelling chili sauce she had simmering on the stove. Looking me up and down, she asked suspiciously, "Where did you get those glad rags?"

The tone of her voice took the wind out of my sails. "I sold my watch to Winn for twenty dollars," I said.

"Well, that's scandalous!" Mum banged the pot lid down with a puff of steam. "It's plain highway robbery. That Bulova was worth twice that much, and what's more, Winn knows it. Wait till I see that girl. I'll give her a piece of my mind." She did too, but Winn and I stuck to our bargain.

Dad had sent several copies of the newspaper up to Aunt Aggie. Her letter of congratulations almost made me cry.

You've made me the proudest woman in Muskoka County, she wrote glowingly. *And just think, when you're a little old lady and I'm long since pushing up daisies, you'll look at that beautiful Bulova and remember your Aunt Aggie. I wish your grandpa could have read your story. The old curmudgeon used to say I was only good for digging potatoes. I guess he was disappointed in me for not getting married and having children. But if I had, I couldn't have become the "bravest man you know," now could I?*

But Aunt Aggie was alone in her admiration of me. Ruthie Vaughan told everybody I was absolutely obnoxious. Ada-May called me insufferable. Even Glad had finally deserted me for a new friend. But worst of all, I heard through the grapevine that Lorne Huntley said I was an agonizing bore. And Georgie Dunn, the stupid drip, was going around with goofy old Wanda again.

Then Sylvia Lamont, a new girl in third form who hadn't had time to get sick of me yet, told me something that nearly made me die of envy. "I heard that Gloria Carlyle and Lorne Huntley went to the Silver Slipper last Saturday night," she said.

The Silver Slipper was a dance hall built on the side of the South Kingsway hill. It was shaped like a lady's high-heeled shoe. At night its unique shape was outlined with electric lights that glittered through the trees.

"I don't believe it," I snorted. "Who said?"

"Gloria."

"She'd say anything for attention," I muttered.

But I believed it, all right, because Lorne had passed me on the school staircase between periods and had purposely looked the other way. With a heavy heart I remembered that he had half promised, that soft spring night at the Pally, that he would take me to the Slipper someday.

There was nothing left for me to do but throw myself into my work and show them all. So I began to write feverishly, sending stories off pellmell in all directions. Back came the rejections thick and fast. Only one editor had the decency to write me a letter. It was from *Liberty* magazine.

Dear Miss Thomson,

I have read your stories with considerable interest. They are very good for one so young. (I had casually mentioned my age, hoping the editor would think I was a teenage genius like Deanna Durbin.) *However, I regret that your contributions do not meet the high standards of Liberty.*

May I suggest, Miss Thomson, that you further your education before attempting to write professionally? Also, I urge you to aquire a typewriter (a typewriter!) *since handwritten material is seldom read by editors. I hope this advice will be helpful to you and I wish to thank you for sending us your lovely essays. Keep writing and good luck!*

Sincerely,
Joan M. Smith, Editor

With a huge sigh I abandoned my writing career forever.

17

Ostracized

Gloria was having a Hallowe'en party on her sixteenth birthday and she didn't invite me.

"Isn't that just like a witch to be born on Hallowe'en?" I snorted to Glad, who was grudgingly speaking to me again.

If I thought she'd laugh at my joke I had another think coming. She didn't react at all. Right away I got suspicious. "Are you going?" I asked.

"Well — I've been invited," she hedged, not looking me in the eye.

"Yeah, but are you going?"

"I think so," she admitted hesitantly.

"Well!" I huffed indignantly. "With friends like you, who needs enemies!" Then I wheeled around and darted across Jane Street, nearly getting run over by a horse. But actually my sarcasm was just a smoke screen. Inside, my heart was as heavy as lead.

Gradually I found out that not only was "bunch" going, but all our gang from Veeny Street too! Even Arthur.

"I thought you didn't like Gloria," I said reproachfully.

"I don't particularly, but Marjorie Tabbs will be there."

"What about Georgie? Is he going?"

"Of course, stupid. He's taking Wanda."

I nearly choked on the next question. "How about Lorne?"

"Well, what do you think? Gloria's his girlfriend."

I went upstairs, my nose and eyes dripping, and spilled it all out in my diary. I called everybody filthy names and used as many swear words as I could think of. Then I locked it up and hid the key in the knothole in the baseboard.

A couple of days before Hallowe'en I happened to hear Winn and Willa discussing a come-as-you-are party.

"We'd better ask Mum before we make any plans," Willa said. She knew Mum better than Winn did. Mum didn't like unexpected company.

But this time she was surprisingly easy to persuade. "Well, glory be, that sounds like fun," she said. "I don't mind as long as you two are willing to foot the bill."

"Oh, that's no problem, Cousin Fran," Winn assured her. "The boys bring the fruit and pop and the girls make the sandwiches, so it's no hardship for anybody."

Mum thought that was a wonderful arrangement. "I'll bake some banana cupcakes," she volunteered.

Willa sat right down at the dining room table and made out a list. Then Winn phoned everybody and told them what to bring and that it was a "come as you are" party.

"There's fifteen coming altogether, Cousin Fran. Is that okey-doke?"

"Land sakes, that'll be a houseful. But I guess we can manage," Mum agreed.

All this time I'd been sitting on the leather rocking chair in the front room pretending to read *Jane of Lantern Hill*. I had read it four times already so it didn't take much concentration.

I glanced up. Winn and Willa had their heads together going over the list.

"How many boys are coming?" I asked casually.

"Eight. But they're not boys, kiddo, they're men. Archie Bones is the youngest and he's nineteen."

"How many girls?" I tried to sound indifferent.

"Seven, counting Willa and me. Why?"

"Well . . . if I stayed it would make it even."

"I thought you'd be with your own gang, or bunch, or whatever you call them," Willa said.

The sudden lump that came up in my throat made it hard for me to answer. "They're all going to Gloria Carlyle's birthday party and I wasn't invited," I confessed.

"It serves you right!" Arthur was always butting in where he had no business. "The way you've been boasting since you won that darn contest would make a person puke."

Willa shot him a withering glance for using such a disgusting word. Then she said to me, "You *have* been particularly obnoxious lately, Bea. It's no wonder you've been ostracized by your friends."

"I know," I agreed ruefully. "Even Glad is still mad. She's going to Gloria's party too."

Suddenly Winn loomed over me, hands on hips, and peered at me through narrowed eyes. "Do you think it would be humanly possible for you to go through one whole night without mentioning that contest even once?"

"Oh, Winn, I promise. I intend never to mention it again as long as I live."

I knew I'd won when Willa said, "Well, you'd better ask Mum first."

Mum was crying because she was chopping onions for green tomato pickles. "They're too old a crowd for you, Bea." She sniffed and wiped her eyes on her apron. "You should stick to friends your own age."

"You'll make a fool of yourself," predicted Arthur with a smirk. "You're just a kid."

"I won't — I'm not — oh, please, Mum, say it's okay."

"Well, if you'll help me tidy the house without complaints I'll think about it," she said, scraping the onion off the board into the big preserving kettle.

I knew that was as good as yes and I was ecstatic. This would be a real adult party. One that would make Gloria's seem like kid stuff.

The day of the party I worked like a trojan. My jobs were to wash the kitchen and bathroom floors. But no sooner had I finished than Mum got down on her hands and knees and did them all over again to make sure they were spotless. Then she went around holding her heart.

"It's your own fault if your heart hurts, Mum.

Nothing ever suits you," I said crabbily.

"I know." She sat down heavily, fanning herself by flapping her apron up and down.

I felt bad and told her I was sorry.

Next I helped Billy get dressed for shellying-out. It was his first experience, since he'd been sick the two years before, so he was beside himself with excitement. I made him into the cutest pirate with a black eyepatch and charcoal moustache. Jakey wore an old sheet with eyeholes cut in it, so he could scare the daylights out of his little girl friends.

By seven-thirty everything was ready.

Winn came downstairs all gussied up, looking like she'd just stepped out of a band-box. She had tons of rouge and lipstick on.

"I thought this was a 'come as you are' party," I said. "You had on your old housedress and Mum's dust cap when you were phoning."

"Soooo, who's going to know if you don't squeal?"

I raced upstairs, painted my face and put on Willa's peach blouse with my grey flannel skirt. If only I had spectator pumps, I thought, I'd look five years older. Willa frowned when she saw me. "I hope you don't mind, Willa." I crossed my arms to hide the scorched sleeve.

"Oh, I guess not. It's yours now anyway. But if I ever catch you sneaking my clothes again I'll wring your skinny neck."

At last the guests started to arrive. Everybody must have been wearing their Sunday best when Winn phoned because that's what they were all decked out in.

On went the radio and down went the lights.

Luigi Romanelli's band was playing "Oh, Johnny!" and everybody began to dance. I felt a bit shy at first, so I sat in the corner by the Quebec heater. Suddenly a boy (a man — he looked at least twenty-one) took my hand and pulled me to my feet. "Hi, Doll, my name's Bucky White. Wanna dance?"

Bucky White was the spitting image of Tyrone Power. My knees wobbled as he put his arm around my waist. But he was such a smooth dancer that I fell right into step. When the music stopped, he kept his arm around me as if he didn't want to change partners.

"Is that your real name — Bucky?" I asked as we began swaying to the tune of "Now's the Time to Fall in Love."

"Nah. My old lady nicknamed me that when I was a kid and it stuck." He grinned down at me engagingly. "Rupert's my real name. How's that for a monicker?"

"Rupert's a gorgeous name," I said. "My name's Beatrice but my mother calls me Booky. How's that for a monicker?"

"Hey, I think I like that. Booky and Bucky. We should make a great team."

Oh, wow! I thought to myself.

I was having the time of my life. All the men asked me to dance, and halfway through nearly every dance Bucky cut in and took me back again.

Before we knew it a couple of hours had rolled romantically by. We were all stepping lively to a brand new song called "A-Tisket A-Tasket" when Jakey and Billy came bursting into the front door with their loaded Eaton's bags. They dumped their loot on the dining room table, which had been shoved into a corner to make room for dancing. Then, before Mum could stop them, they ran straight out again.

"Greedy little monsters," laughed Winn, popping a jelly baby into her mouth. We all followed suit, helping ourselves as we danced by the table. Pretty soon what had been a big pile was reduced to a few miserable scraps.

It was about nine-thirty when Jakey and Billy straggled in with their second bagful. It wasn't nearly as full as their first. When they saw what had happened to their precious hoard they both flew into a furious rage.

"Grey-eyed greedy guts!" screamed Jakey, his black eyes flashing.

"Greedy guts!" echoed tired little Billy, the tears streaming down his face and washing off his moustache.

Mum came in from the kitchen to see what the fuss was about, and when she saw what we'd done she swept us all with a scathing look, her eyes flashing just like Jakey's.

"Never you mind," she began, wiping their tears with her apron. "I'll fix the lot of them. I'll save the best of the party food for you two, and you can share it in the morning. Now off you go to bed. You look like little lost urchins!"

Then she got her biggest cake tin and filled it to the brim with our most delectable food. But there was plenty left, and we still had a wonderful time. We danced and drank pop and stuffed ourselves right up until midnight. And I never missed a single dance!

As always, Winn was the life of the party, but

Willa was the belle of the ball. Wesley Armstrong had brought a friend by the name of Clifford Best and he and Willa hit it right off. Poor Wesley, he was absolutely desolate. He slipped away early and Willa didn't even notice.

When Arthur came home from Gloria's party we were having our last dance. "Did you have fun?" I called over Bucky's broad shoulder.

"Drop dead!" Arthur snarled and he headed straight upstairs.

Later, when Glad and I made up again, she told me Marjorie Tabbs had snubbed Arthur all night and he'd had to settle for Ada.

The next night, right after supper, Billy hopped down from the table, grabbed his grubby Eaton's bag off the chair and headed for the door.

"Whoa there, young fella!" Dad caught him by the tail of his sweater. "Where are you off to?"

"Shellying-out, o'course," Billy said with a grin.

"Dummy!" sneered Jakey, twirling his finger above his head to show how dizzy Billy was. "Hallowe'en's over, stoopid! Don't you know nothing?"

Poor Billy was crestfallen and embarrassed. Tears spurting from his eyes, he hightailed it down to the cellar to hide in the coal bin, our laughter echoing after him.

*   *   *

The holiday season that year was both happy and sad. Christmas was a madhouse at the Nuthouse, but it was worth it because I could afford to buy everybody a swell present. I bought Dad a set of Westinghouse tubes for the radio, and Mum a picture of a rose-covered cottage in a gold frame. Superimposed on it was her favourite poem: "It takes a heap of livin' to make a house a home." They were both thrilled.

New Year's Day was nice too. We were all invited to Uncle Charlie's and Aunt Myrtle's for a chicken dinner. Then a week later came the sad part.

Winn had to move away. She'd been promoted to head cashier in a new Loblaw's Groceteria in Birch-cliff. Birchcliff was at the opposite end of the city from Swansea, so she had to find another place to live.

She had tears in her eyes when she told us. "My grandma used to say, 'Be careful what you wish for, for you might get it.' Now I know what she meant," she lamented, carefully packing her things.

"I'm sorry you have to go, Winn," I said sincerely. I didn't tell her I'd be happy to get my half of the bed back. It would be heavenly to be able to roll over again.

We all loved Winn. Jakey even got into a fist fight with one of his chums because the boy said Winn wasn't really his sister and Jakey swore she was. He was really proud of the black eye he got to prove it too.

Billy cried when she kissed him goodbye, so she gave him a nickel to make him stop. He had found out recently what money was for.

Dolefully we stood together at the front room window watching Winn trudging up the street with her grip. She turned and waved and we all waved back, banging on the window. Then she bent her head against the cold north wind, and hanging onto her hat with her free hand, disappeared up Veeny Street in a swirl of snow.

It was strange, I thought as I wandered around the house after she left, how one person's leaving could make a place seem so empty.

18
Caught in the act

One bleak winter evening I was feeling especially lonely for Winn. I had found that sometimes when I was upset about something it helped to tell it to my diary. It had become like a true friend. It was even more trustworthy than Glad, since it couldn't talk and tell my secrets. The little book was already crammed full and I'd had to add a sheaf of pages at the end.

I went upstairs and felt for the key in the knothole. It wasn't there! Panic-stricken, I dashed downstairs. "Hey!" I yelled. "Who stole the key to my diary?"

"Hay's for horses," grunted Arthur.

"Who'd want to steal it, for pity's sake?" muttered Willa. She'd been kind of crabby ever since Winn left.

"Hold your tong!" Dad barked. "We're trying to listen to a good play about the war of 1812."

"You probably mislaid it, Bea." Mum didn't look up from the sock she was darning, stretched over a light bulb.

"I didn't mislay it! I always keep it in — in a

special place. It's full of my private thoughts and whoever stole it is a criminal. There's a law against invasion of privacy, you know!"

"Get upstairs and look for it. You'll find it right where you left it." Dad gave me a fierce glare. If looks could kill I'd be dead, I thought as I stomped back up the stairs.

At the top of the staircase I happened to notice the sound of exaggerated snoring coming from the boys' room. Jakey had been sent to bed early without his supper for breaking a window in the school basement with his slingshot.

When I heard the phony snore I said to myself, "Aha!" Creeping into the room, I stood as still as a statue beside Jakey's bed. Billy was asleep beside him, his head under the bedclothes. Jakey's eyes were squeezed shut and he let out another loud snore. Then he gradually opened one eye a crack. When he saw me standing there he nearly jumped out of his skin. I snarled viciously, "Jakey! You brat! Where's my key?"

His dark eyes were wide open now, shining brazenly in the light from the hallway. He didn't answer, so I grabbed him by the nightshirt and yanked him to a sitting position. "If you don't fess up" — my lips were just inches from his nose — "I'll pinch you black and blue."

He felt under his flat pillow and came up with the little gold key. I snatched it out of his hand. "How dare you invade my privacy? Don't you know you could go to jail for that?"

I could tell by the impudent look on his face that he didn't believe a word of it. Now that he was a husky ten-year-old he wasn't too easily scared. He wasn't even afraid of Dad anymore. Only yesterday Dad had chased him, hell bent for leather, down the yard waving a gad in his hand. Jakey had leaped like a jack-rabbit to the top of the board fence and from there to the woodshed roof. Dancing around the flat roof like a whirling dervish, he had looked so comical that even Dad had to laugh, so he got away scot-free.

"How much of my diary did you read?" I demanded ferociously, tightening my grip on the neck of his nightshirt until he started to gag. "Tell me or I'll go downstairs this minute and call the police."

"I read it all!" he choked, still defiant, but looking a bit scared now. "And if you let go my nightshirt, Bea, I'll tell you something good."

"Good! What could a sneak thief say that's good?"

"Your diary was just like reading a real book, Bea."

That was the last thing I expected to hear, and it took the wind right out of my sails. So Jakey rushed on. "I liked it even better than *The Western Boy* by Horatio Alger and you know how famous he is."

Such a huge compliment made me suspicious again. "What were you doing in our room anyway?" I asked, still using a menacing voice, but loosening my hold on his nightshirt.

"I was just hollering out the window at Wally. He wanted to know why I couldn't come out and play dibs. Then the knothole popped out all by itself, so I got curious and stuck my finger in just for fun. Then I found the key so I thought I might as well hunt up your diary. But I didn't intend to read it all, Bea, honest. Only once I started I couldn't stop. It's a swell story, Bea. I bet you could make it into a book."

By this time I was completely disarmed. I let go his nightshirt and he fell back onto the pillow. "I'm sorry, Bea," he said.

I'd never heard Jakey apologize before. At least not to me. And his big brown eyes shone with sincerity.

"You mean it, Jakey?"

"About being sorry?"

"No. About my diary being more interesting than *The Western Boy*."

"Sure. The part about Aunt Susan chasing the thief down Yonge Street made me laugh my head off."

This tickled me pink and I had to smile. "Okay, I believe you. But Jakey, I want you to promise me something."

"What?"

"That you won't tell any of your friends about it, okay? They're my private thoughts and I don't want them spread all over Swansea."

"Okay, I promise." Jakey crossed his heart. Then he slid his hand under his pillow again and pulled out my diary!

"Jakey! You brat! You've got more nerve than a canal horse."

He laughed and said, "Night, Bea!"

"Night, Jakey." I gave him a pretend punch on the chin.

"Don't let the bedbugs bite!" chirped a squeaky voice from under the covers.

"Billy! How long have you been awake?" I demanded.

"You just woke me up now," he answered plaintively.

"Go to sleep, both of you," I said and shut the door.

When I was ready for bed, I opened my diary. But instead of writing in it, I started to read it from page one, November 9, 1937.

Jakey was right! It was a swell story. It made me laugh and it made me cry. I decided then and there I *was* going to be a writer, no matter what.

19
Easter

Easter Sunday fell on April 9 that year. The day was as warm as toast, so right after church Glad and Ruth and Ada and I went down to the boardwalk to show off our new spectator pumps. When I got home a few hours later a heavenly aroma was filling the kitchen.

"Mmmm. What's for supper, Mum?" Jakey came into the kitchen at the same time I did.

"Roast pork, butter fries and tapioca pudding. How does that suit Your Majesty?" Turning towards him, she let out a shriek. "In heaven's name, child, what have you done to yourself?"

Jakey's saucy face was littered with red-dotted bits of toilet paper. "I needed a shave," he said solemnly.

"Have you taken leave of your senses?" Mum scolded. "You're only eleven years old. Arthur only shaves once a week and he's eighteen."

"Is that why the girls call you 'Peaches,' Arthur?" I snickered.

"Get lost, Bea," he snapped.

"Did you use your father's straight razor?" demanded Mum, wetting the flannel and wiping the blood none too gently off Jakey's face.

"Sure," he admitted, not even flinching as she dabbed each cut with stinging peroxide. "And I sharpened it on his strop too. I'd better tell him to be careful."

"You'd better keep your mouth shut if you know what's good for you," warned Arthur.

I could tell by the weird look on his face he was remembering the worst beating he ever got with the razor strop. It was the day he had set the toilet paper on fire. Mum had gone to the dentist's to get a gumboil lanced and the dentist had just injected the novocaine when Mum got a "flash" of disaster. Leaping out of the chair, she ran all the way home with the white bib still around her neck and raced upstairs just in time to douse the flaming bathroom curtains. Dad had stropped Arthur so hard he cried all night and had to sit on a pillow for a week. Mum and Dad had had a terrible row about that. And Dad never hit Arthur again.

"Aww," Jakey answered, smart-alecky, "Dad don't strop Billy nor me."

That was true. Mum said he was getting soft in his old age, but personally I think he'd learned his lesson.

Just then Billy came up from the cellar sniffing the air. "You're the best cooker in the whole world, Mum," he said.

"Oh, pshaw, I bet you say that to all the girls," teased Mum, pinching his nose.

Then she called Willa to lay the table in the dining room, because Easter was a special day. Her good mood was contagious and there was a happy feeling in the house. "Too bad Winn isn't here," she said to no one in particular.

Just then Dad came in the back door. He'd been across the road talking to Gladie's father when we came home. Ignoring everybody, including Jakey, he went right into the front room and switched on the radio. When the tubes warmed up we could hear the faint chiming of a clock.

"That's Big Ben from London," Dad said loud enough for all of us to hear. He recognized the sound because he had stood under the famous clock to have his picture taken during the Great War.

We all paused to listen, sort of reverently. Then Big Ben stopped bonging and some faraway voices started chanting, "Stop Hitler! Stop Hitler! Stop Hitler!" Then another station floated in and drowned out the fearful chant with the lilting tune, "In your Easter bonnet . . ."

Mum stood in the doorway between the kitchen and the dining room bunching up her apron in nervous fingers. "I knew it!" she cried. "There's another war coming. Oh, how I wish you were younger, Arthur."

Arthur acted as if he didn't even hear her. "If England goes to war with Germany, Dad, will Canada go too?" he asked eagerly.

This time Dad didn't even try to deny the likelihood of another war. "There's no doubt about it." He nodded gravely. "If it comes to that it'll be our bounden duty to fight for king and country. And that's the long and short of it, Arthur."

"I don't want to hear another word!" Mum went back to the stove and started banging pots and pans.

"If men had the sense of fishing worms," she ranted, "there wouldn't be any wars."

Suddenly the Easter spirit had been snuffed out like a candle. Then, just as suddenly, the front door flew open.

"Hello the house!" came a cheerful greeting. It was Winn, looking fresh as a daisy in her new Easter rig-out.

"Winn! Winn!" we all cried in unison. We hadn't seen hide nor hair of her since New Year's. And her timely visit was like the sun breaking through on a cloudy day.

"Well, for land's sake, speak of the devil!" Mum wiped her hands on her apron and gave our favourite cousin a big bear-hug. "We've got lots to eat, Winn, so why don't you take off your hat and stay a while?"

"Why don't you stay all night, Winn? I'll lend you my side of the bed," I volunteered happily.

"Yeah, Winn, stay! Stay! Stay!" begged Billy and Jakey.

Winn looked herself up and down. "Well, by cracky" — she always knew all the latest slang — "I don't know what I've got . . . but whatever it is I should bottle it and make a fortune."

Laughing, she took off her hat and coat and hung them on the hall tree. Then she handed Billy and Jakey each a purple box with a yellow chicken pictured on it. Inside, nested in a bed of green shredded cellophane, was a huge Laura Secord Easter egg, the kind with the creamy filling and the yellow yolk in the middle.

They squealed their thanks and Mum cried, "Now don't you two eat a bite before supper. I haven't been slaving all day over a hot stove just to have you turn your noses up."

"Oh, don't worry, Mum," Jakey said, testing the heft of the egg in his hand. "I'm so hungry I could eat a horse."

"Me too!" echoed Billy. For once they agreed on something.

Willa hadn't been able to get a word in edgewise, but she had a smile on her face as she set another place at the table. Winn and Willa were best friends, as well as cousins, just like Glad and me.

Billy begged to sit beside Winn at the table, so just for fun (trust Winn to play a joke on somebody) she switched his china dinner plate for a glass one. We all knew why. Billy had a bad habit of hiding his crusts under the rim of his plate, and try as she might, Mum hadn't been able to break him of it.

He was so chirpy with excitement, perched on the telephone book beside Winn, that he didn't even notice the transparent plate until the bread crusts tucked around the edge showed right through. Realizing he'd been tricked, he threw a tantrum right at the table. Dad didn't even bat an eye. He sure had changed! Either that or his mind was far away — somewhere in France, maybe, about twenty-two years ago.

"Oh, for pity's sake, child, stop your caterwauling. You're enough to try the patience of a saint." Mum jumped up and whisked the plate, crusts and all, off the table and replaced it with an ordinary one.

When Billy settled down again Winn said, "I was just pulling your leg, Billy-bo-bingo. Give us a kiss to make up."

Billy was pouting, trying to stay mad, but in spite of himself he started to giggle. Then he puckered his lips and lifted his face for her kiss. His childish laughter was infectious and pretty soon we all joined in.

And the war clouds that had seeped into our house through the airwaves were blown away by Easter joy.

20

Dear Diary

Dear Diary,

So much happened in Toronto today that I thought I'd better record it for posterity. (I wonder if anybody will read these words after I'm dead? Mum says when she has a creepy feeling like that it's as if someone just walked over her grave.) Anyway, the biggest event of the day was the visit of King George and Queen Elizabeth to our fair city. The only disappointment was that they didn't bring the little princesses with them.

Glad and Ada and I went down to the Exhibition Grounds to see them. Ruth couldn't come because her little brother, Wally, has scarlet fever and they've got a red quarantine sign tacked on their front door. Mum says they won't be allowed to poke their noses out for a least three weeks. I sure hope we don't get it!

The three of us managed to find a spot that wasn't too crowded, and we sat on our coats and waited for ages. Mum would have had a fit if she'd seen me sitting on my new spring coat. But it was worth it.

KING ABDICATES, YORK SUCCEEDS
All British Dominions Give Assent

EDWARD, ABDICATING SAYS 'CAN NO LONGER DISCHARGE HEAVY TASK'

'I Am Going To Marry Mrs. Simpson,' Am Prepared To Go' He Is Quoted

HOME AND SPORT EDITION

'EVERYTHING INDICATES MARRIAGE IS THE IDEA' SAYS CANNES' FRIEND

SAY KING WILL BE PLAIN MR. WINDSOR

AIR OF MYSTERY

BRITISH EMPIRE'S NEW SOVEREIGNS

AWESOME HUSH FILLS HOUSE AS KING RENOUNCES THRONE

NEW KING'S TOUR TO BE 'ALBERT I'

SCENE IS DRAMATIC

CANADA TO ACCEPT KING'S ABDICATION

TO CELEBRATE BIRTHDAY AS NEW KING OF ENGLAND

'PLANE LINE EDWARD'S LEAVES FROM HENDON

DONATIONS TO STAR SANTA CLAUS FUND

DOCTOR, WRITERS WOUNDED AS REBELS CRASH 'PLANE

YOUNG BOB FELLER STAYS AT CLEVELAND

TELL OF ATTACK

EMPIRE STANDS UNSHAKEN SIR WILLIAM MULOCK SAYS

INDICATES EDWARD WILL LEAVE SOON

SACRIFICES COVETED HAT FOR SISTER IN HOSPITAL

'COLDER TO-NIGHT' SAYS WEATHERMAN

FIFTY INTERESTED IN ELECTRIC TRAIN

THE WEATHER

DEATH NOTICES

First came the Mounties in their red uniforms, sitting straight as arrows on the backs of their black horses. Those beautiful animals are so well trained that even a couple of stray dogs nipping at their heels didn't make them miss a step.

At last came the moment we had been waiting for — Their Imperial Majesties gliding by in an open limousine. The shiny black Rolls Royce was only travelling about two miles an hour so everybody got a good look. I wonder what it's like to be on display like that? It is hard to believe that they are merely flesh-and-blood human beings like the rest of us, who eat and clean their teeth and go to the bathroom. Arthur says they don't even dress themselves or comb their own hair. But I imagine they get to go to the bathroom privately.

Anyway, the limousine was moving along so slowly that before the Mounties could do anything about it a man broke from the crowd, jumped on the running board, stuck out his hand and shouted, "Hi, King!" This upset the Mounties no end, but His Majesty didn't seem to mind a bit. He just smiled and shook the man's hand and answered politely, "I'm fine. How are you?"

I was so close I actually heard him speak. He has a gorgeous English accent and his voice sounds much nicer than it does on the radio in his Christmas message to the Empire. Also, he is much handsomer than his pictures. He has a nice suntan (it must be warmer in England than it is here) and marvellous white teeth. (Arthur says no wonder, he has his own private dentist. I don't know where he gets all his information from.)

I couldn't see the Queen too well because she was waving and bobbing her blue hat to the people on the other side. But the King happened to wave and smile directly at us and for a fleeting second his deep blue eyes met mine. It was a thrilling moment but Glad spoiled it by insisting he had been looking straight at her. Then Ada said we were both wrong, the King's attention had been riveted right on her. Honestly, dear diary, I am continually amazed at how unobservant the average person is. I guess that's because I'm gifted with an eye for detail. Born writers are noted for that.

When it was over we caught the streetcar at the Dufferin gates. It was packed solid with people all buzzing with excitement over the great event. One woman cried ecstatically, "Imagine. We have just witnessed history!" and her friend replied, also ecstatically, "Now I can die happy!"

Nearby two men started to argue. "They didn't come all the way over here for nothing," growled the tall one.

"What d'ya mean by that?" the other man, who was short and stocky and mean looking, growled right back.

Just then the streetcar gave a big lurch and the short man bumped smack into the tall one's stomach, knocking the wind out of him. Glowering down at the smaller man, he said, "I mean they come here to drum up patriotism, that's what. Next thing you know us Canucks'll be singing 'Pack Up Your Troubles in Your Old Kit Bag' again."

Then the short one stuck out his chest and declared belligerently, "Well, I for one would be proud to fight for king and country."

127

The tall one sneered, "Would you, now? Well, I say let them damn limeys fight their own battles. I lost a brother in the last war and I ain't about to lose a son in the next one."

When the little man dared to mutter "coward" under his breath, all heck broke loose. All the men on the streetcar started yelling and punching each other, but the crowd was so thick nobody had room to fall down. Glad and Ada and I were lucky to be sitting on the circular seat at the back out of harm's way.

Suddenly the streetcar jolted to a stop and the motorman jumped out and hailed a policeman. As luck would have it, a Black Maria was parked right beside the curb. So the crowd shoved the two men who had started the ruckus out the doors and the policemen hustled them into the back of the Black Maria, jabbing them with their billies.

I've never seen anything like that happen in Toronto before. I guess that's why our city is nicknamed "Toronto the good." Anyway, the three of us could hardly wait to get home to tell about it.

But the minute we turned down Veeny Street we knew something was wrong. Mum was running up one side of the street and Aunt Ellie was running down the other. They were both shouting at the top of their lungs, "Billy! Billy! Billy!"

Well, dear diary, my blood ran cold. Terrible visions of my little brother drowned or killed or kidnapped flashed through my mind. "What's wrong? What's happened?" the three of us yelled.

Mum screamed hysterically, "Billy's lost! He's been gone for hours. Oh, the good Lord have mercy! If only I hadn't spanked him yesterday for stealing buns *off the baker's wagon. Maybe that's why he's run off."*

"Call the police! Call the police!" I screeched. Then Arthur announced they already had. His face was the colour of a soda biscuit.

Aunt Ellie had to practically carry Mum over to her house to try to calm her down. Mum kept crying, "Oh, my baby! My little Billy-bo-bingo. If the dear Lord brings you back to me I'll never lay a hand on you again."

Arthur and I sat on our front stoop, panic-stricken. There was nothing we could do but pray, so I said right out loud, "God, if you bring Billy home safe and sound I'll never miss church again," and Arthur added, "Amen!"

Jakey came up the walk and sat on the bottom step. His eyes were bright with fear. "I'm not going to punch Billy anymore," he promised solemnly.

We lapsed into silence. Then about five minutes later a police car came cruising down the street and stopped in front of our house. And who should hop out, all smiles, his face smeared with chocolate, but Billy-bo-bingo.

Mum and Aunt Ellie came hightailing it across the road and Mum swooped Billy up in her arms. First she hugged him, then she hit him, then she hugged him, then she hit him. The poor little guy was completely bewildered. "Ow, Mum! Ow, Mum! Whatcha doin' that for?" he cried.

At last Mum got hold of herself, and setting Billy down, she grabbed his chin in a tight squeeze and made him look at her. His blue eyes were as big as saucers. "Where have you been, young man?" she demanded. "I've nearly been out of my mind. Just wait

till your father comes home! Where have you been?
Answer me."

"Gee whiz, Mum" — Billy rubbed his bottom and
stared in confusion at the crowd gathering around
him — "I just went to see the King like everybody else."

The policeman filled in the story. Billy had
walked along Bloor Street all the way to Lansdowne
Avenue (about eight miles from home) looking for the
King. There a woman found him crying and took him
to the police station.

"Why didn't you tell the police your name and
address?" Arthur asked. Nobody else had even
thought of that.

"'Cause if I told, I'd get found too fast and I
wanted more ice cream," explained Billy. When Mum
heard that it was all she could do not to smack him
again.

Well, all's well that ends well, as Grampa used to
say. I've got to go to sleep now. I'm dog tired. What a
day!

B.M.T.

May 18, 1939
In today's pink Tely there was a full-page report of
Their Majesties' visit and a beautiful picture of the
Queen with the Dionne quintuplets. Apparently the
Queen had especially asked to see them. In the photo-
graph she's leaning over and smiling down at the five
little angels just as proudly as if they were her own.
Which they practically are since they've been made
wards of the Crown.

On the next page there was a long column about the big fight on the Dufferin streetcar and the arrest of the two culprits.

Of course there wasn't a word about a little boy who was lost for hours searching for the King. If I was a reporter that's the story I would have written.

B.M.T.

21

The end of school

June came, and wonder of wonders, I passed again.
Now that I had my commercial diploma I decided to
hunt for a permanent job.

"I'm proud as punch of you, Bea," Mum said as
she scanned my final report card, "but I still wish you
had a little more education." She wanted so much for
all of her children to be well educated. It had haunted
her all her life that she'd never gone to high school.

"Well, Mum" — it was nearly supper time, so I
got the plates down from the kitchen cabinet and slid
them around the oilcloth as if I was dealing cards —
"don't forget I'll be seventeen in November. You were
only fourteen when you started work at Eaton's." I set
a glass full of spoons in the middle of the table.
"Besides, I want some new clothes and a permanent
wave. I think I'll go downtown tomorrow and fill out
an application at Eaton's."

Mum's brow furrowed as she poked the carrots
with a fork. "Well, if you must go to work, Eaton's is
the best firm to work for." She was a dyed-in-the-wool
Eatonian.

So the next day I applied for a job at Eaton's. Then, afterwards, since it was a nice warm day, I decided to go window shopping up Yonge Street. I stopped in front of Loew's Theatre to look at scenes from the picture playing there, *Lucky Night,* starring Myrna Loy and Robert Taylor.

Suddenly, from behind me, a voice that was so close it seemed to come out of my hair whispered, "Wanna buy a duck?" It was a perfect imitation of Joe Penner, the comedian. I only knew one person who could do that. I spun around and sure enough it was Lorne Huntley. "What are you doing downtown all by your lonesome?" he asked, looking as handsome as Robert Taylor himself.

"I just applied for a job at Eaton's," I answered proudly.

"How would you like to go to the pictures?" he asked, inclining his head toward the ticket box.

"No thanks, I've already seen it." The second the words left my mouth I could have bitten my tongue off. Imagine missing a chance to go to the pictures with Robert Taylor . . . I mean Lorne Huntley.

But he surprised me by saying, "Okay, how about George Brent and Bette Davis? They're at the Tivoli in *Dark Victory.*

So off we went, hand in hand, around the corner to the Tivoli. The show was marvellous, but the newsreel — *The Eyes and Ears of the World* — was really scary. It showed Adolf Hitler reviewing his troops, children in England being taught how to use gas masks, fighting on the borders of Albania (wherever that is), and dead soldiers lying on the ground.

"I hope we get into the war soon," whispered

Lorne. Our heads were almost touching because he had his arm across the back of my seat. "I'm going to be an air gunner." An air gunner! The very words sent shivers up my spine.

But once outside in the sunlight again I soon forgot the bad news because Lorne asked me to have supper with him at a fancy restaurant called Muirhead's. I was so unused to restaurants that I didn't know what to do. So Lorne ordered for both of us. "Cordon Bleu for two," he told the waitress. I'd never even heard of it before.

We didn't talk much, but whenever I glanced up, Lorne was watching me. His grey eyes were twinkling, and the way his long dimples creased his cheeks made him look the spittin' image of Gary Cooper. I couldn't for the life of me figure out what a homely girl like me was doing downtown in a fancy restaurant having supper with a boy who looked exactly like a motion picture star.

The next surprise came when he led me right past the streetcar stop and around the corner to a parking lot. Swaggering over to a shiny blue car, he patted its hood lovingly.

"Who's car is it?" I asked nervously. What if the owner came along and caught us touching his car?

"It's mine . . . who else's?" he answered with a big self-satisfied grin. "It's a 1932 Chevy roadster in perfect condition," he explained as we circled around it. "It's got everything — celluloid side curtains that snap on in winter, a roof that folds back in summer and a rumble seat that's hardly ever been used."

He yanked open the rumble seat and sure

enough the brown leather shone like new. "The sales-
man told me it used to belong to a little old lady who
only drove it on Sundays," he said proudly. Then he
swooped his hand like Sir Galahad and invited me to
hop in.

The inside was as perfect as the outside. "Did
your dad buy it for you?" I asked naively.

"You must be joking." He scowled, and I wished I
hadn't asked. "My old man wouldn't give me an apple
for an orchard. I had to work for it, in his factory. I've
been so busy lately I haven't had time to call anybody.
Not even you."

What a perfect excuse! "It sure is a beauty. What's this for?" I touched a knob on the front panel. Without answering he turned the knob and in a minute the radio warmed up and started playing "My Blue Heaven." The song seemed to suit our mood to a T as we took off up Yonge Street.

"Are you cold?" he asked.

I wasn't, but something told me to say I was. So he flipped a switch and on came the heater full blast.

"Didn't I tell you Demetrius had everything?" he bragged.

"Demetrius?"

"Yeah. That's her name."

Imagine a car with a name! It sounded like a masculine name to me but I didn't mention it.

Lorne drove like an expert, shifting gears and manoeuvring in and out of the streetcar tracks. "Have you got a driving licence?" I asked.

"No. I'll probably get it next week," he answered confidently. That was good enough for me. I was proud as punch sitting beside him, the radio blaring and the streetcar behind us ding-ding-dinging its bell. The heater was burning my knees and the wind was tangling my hair, but I thought blissfully, "Boy! I wouldn't call the king my uncle!"

As we passed High Park and got closer to Swansea I leaned out the window in hopes of seeing somebody I knew to shout at. But I didn't, so I asked Lorne to go down Durie Street and stop at Aunt Milly's. She and Uncle Mort were sitting out on their front stoop. They both jumped up and came to admire Lorne's car. I could tell Aunt Milly took to Lorne instantly by the way she batted her eyelashes and squeezed my arm. Uncle Mort said the car was a jim-dandy, which pleased Lorne no end.

By the time we got parked in front of my house it was quite dark. The radio was playing "My Blue Heaven" again.

We looked at each other in the pale light of the street lamp. "That must be our song," Lorne said, and my heart skipped a beat. Then he suddenly grabbed my hand and blurted out, "Bea . . . have you got a boyfriend?"

Georgie Dunn was the first name I thought of. We'd been "going around" off and on ever since we were kids. But he was Arthur's best friend, so he seemed more like a brother than a boyfriend. Besides, he only owned a bicycle! Then Jimmy Hobbs came to mind, but he hadn't even answered my last letter and that was weeks ago. And there was Bucky White. I'd been to the pictures with him a few times. He had a car too, but it was only an old flivver that had to be cranked. Anyway, he'd met a girl about nineteen or twenty who looked like Ann Southern, and had dropped me like a hot potato. Only my pride was hurt, because I didn't like Bucky much. He was always making jokes about how dumb girls are. I told him if he thought he was so smart he ought to try matching wits with Winn or Willa.

"Well?" Lorne interrupted my thoughts. "Have you?"

"Not right now," I said.

"Bea . . ." His voice became suddenly shy like Jimmy Stewart's.

"What?" Mine went all husky like Jean Arthur's.

"Will you be my girl?"

"Yes," I said before he had a chance to think it over.

Then he tried to kiss me and we bumped noses. We both laughed self-consciously and tried again. This time we succeeded. I had never been kissed like that before. It was like the first sip from a glass of honeydew.

I stood on the sidewalk as he started the engine, put the car in gear and spun away. "Goodnight, sweetheart!" he yelled out the window.

Sweetheart! What a gorgeous word!

When the car had disappeared in a cloud of Veeny Street dust, I hurried into the house and up the stairs two at a time. Getting my diary from my drawer, I took it to the bathroom and latched the door. Then I sat on the toilet lid and wrote shakily:

June 15, 1939

Dear Diary,
I think I'm in love!

22
War clouds

On September 10, 1939, I started my first full-time job at Eaton's. And on the same momentous day Canada declared war on Germany. I was dying to tell somebody about the happenings of my first day at work, but the war news made everything else seem trivial.

At the corner of Yonge and Queen streets a newsboy yelled out the awful headlines: "Canada declares war! Young men flock to volunteer. Read all about it!"

In the few minutes it took for the streetcar to come he sold all his papers. A hush fell over the crowd as they anxiously scanned the front page. You could feel the tension in the air.

"I only hope it's over before Arthur is twenty-one," Mum was saying as I came in the door.

"Do you think the war will last until I'm big enough to go, Mum?" asked Jakey hopefully.

"Don't talk nonsense," she snapped. "It's not you I'm worried about."

"How about me, Mum?" piped up Billy.

"No, son. It won't affect you boys. It's our Arthur I'm fretting about."

Folding the newspaper inside out, as if to make the dreaded truth disappear, she began to mash the potatoes viciously. "Oh, pshaw, they're burnt!" she declared as a few black specks appeared. "Willa won't touch them now."

"Add some pepper, Mum, and she might not notice," I suggested.

She sprinkled a pinch of coarse black pepper on.

"Mum," I said.

"What is it, Bea?" She poured too much milk into the potatoes and made them mushy. "Drat!" she exlaimed. "Willa loathes wet potatoes."

"Mum," I repeated.

"What *is* it, Bea?" She was beginning to sound impatient.

"Can I tell you about my job now?"

"I'm listening."

"Well, I thought I was going to be a salesgirl in the store, but I'm not. I'm a stuffer in the D.A. office."

"For mercy sakes, what's a stuffer?"

"A stuffer stuffs bills into ledgers," I explained. "And I had to pass a typing test too."

"What's typing got to do with stuffing?" At last I'd caught Mum's interest.

"Well, the forelady said it might come in handy if I ever start to climb the ladder."

"What ladder?" asked Jakey. He was sprawled on the worn linoleum floor colouring a map of the world.

"The ladder of success," I told him importantly. "It means that I might get promoted to operator some day."

"I wish you had more schooling," Mum lamented.

"I don't need it, Mum. Miss Barlow — that's my forelady — says I'm well qualified for the job."

Just then Arthur came in the door. He had obtained his senior matriculation in June and had been out job hunting ever since. Usually he came home down at the mouth, but today he was elated. "Mum!" he announced excitedly, "I'm going to join the navy!"

"Over my dead body!" she barked.

"But all the fellas are volunteering, Mum. Don't you know there's a war on?"

"I can read," she returned bitterly. "But you're only nineteen so you'll need my permission and I won't give it. Do you hear?"

Dad and Willa came in. "Dad"—Arthur turned away from Mum — "I'm thinking of joining the navy."

"Well, I don't know much about sailoring, Arthur, but a soldier's life is no bed of roses, I can tell you that firsthand." Dad opened his dinner pail and broke a leftover gingersnap in half for Billy and Jakey. Then he put his thermos to soak in salt water at the tin sink. "Still, if it comes to fighting for king and country you'll be obliged to serve, same as me."

"Not if I have anything to say about it," snapped Mum.

Dad and Arthur exchanged a secret glance. Then Jakey jumped up to show Dad his map and they dropped the gritty subject. "See all them pink countries, Dad?" Jakey pointed them out. "They all belong to England."

"That's right." Dad nodded. "The sun never sets on the British Empire."

Supper was ready so we all sat down glumly at

the table. Sure enough, Willa wouldn't touch the potatoes. I was dying to talk about my job, but I knew it would have to wait until another time.

23
A small brown envelope

The D.A. office (that's what everybody called Eaton's Deposit Accounts office) was on the fifth floor, a huge room with a high ceiling held up by big cement posts. It was jammed full of girls clacking typewriters and men giving orders. A glassed-in corner of the room was the office of the boss, Mr. Bentley. Mr. Bentley was a white-haired, cross-looking man with stooped shoulders and a permanent frown. Every fifteen minutes, like clockwork, he came out of his sanctuary and pussyfooted between the rows of bookkeeping machines, spying from around the posts at the nervous operators.

We stuffers sat sideways on swivel chairs beside the operators, stuffing as fast as our fingers would fly. Mine wouldn't fly fast enough. "You won't last long here if you don't get a move on," warned my operator. So I tried to go faster, but my fingers were all thumbs.

Every time Mr. Bentley popped out from behind a post I nearly jumped out of my skin. "The more hurry the less speed, Miss Thomson," he remarked coldly. He prided himself on knowing all the workers by name no matter how new or insignificant they were.

After he slunk back into his cubicle, Miss Barlow leaned over my shoulder and whispered kindly, "Don't pay him too much mind, Beatrice. His bark is worse than his bite."

I calmed down after that and pretty soon I picked up speed and began popping the bills between the yellow pages as quick as you could say "Jack Robinson."

A few days later I met a girl named Anne Davidson, another stuffer. She had red-gold hair, green eyes, golden lashes and a nice neat nose. In other words, she was beautiful. But she was also nice, which saved me from being too jealous. That and the fact that she said she'd trade her red hair and green eyes for my blonde hair and blue eyes any day of the week. She didn't mention my nose.

"I wish our job didn't have such a stupid name," complained Anne as we sat together in the crowded lunchroom. "It sounds as if we stuff feathers into pillows."

"Or breadcrumbs into turkeys," I laughed, munching on a black-flecked mashed-potato sandwich.

That very afternoon, as if wishing had made it so, Mr. Bentley came out of his glass office, clapped for attention and pompously announced that from that day forward we stuffers would be known as filing clerks.

The title had such a superior ring to it that I could hardly wait to tell somebody. So on my way home I stopped off at Aunt Milly's. Sunny came out the front door with his hoop and stick. "Hi, Bea," he said. "Ma's in the kitchen." Then he rolled the hoop down the stick and ran lickety-split after it.

So I went right in and down the hall to the kitchen. Aunt Milly was sitting with her feet crossed on a chair, balancing one high-heeled slipper on the tip of her big toe and sipping from her favourite green bottle.

"Halloo, there, love!" She slipped her shoe back on and jumped up to fetch me a frosty Coke from the ice box. "Here, sit yourself down and take a load off your feet. Morty's gone for fish and chips, so why don't you stay and have a bite with us?"

"I'd like to, Aunt Milly, but I'm in a hurry to get home."

"Well, what's up? You look like the cat that swallowed the canary."

So I told her all about my life as a filing clerk. Her dark eyes sparkled as she listened to my exaggerated tales. Then she tilted her head back and drained the bottle with a long, satisfied "Ahhhh!"

Suddenly she became quite serious. "I'm tickled pink you like your job, Bea," she said, as she slid the vinegar bottle and salt-cellar onto the chipped enamelled table top. "It'll be good experience for you working downtown in the big city. But don't lose sight of your dreams, Bea. Hitch your wagon to a star. Remember what I've always told you — you're special. You've got a little bit of 'it' and you got it from your Aunt Milly!" She always said that.

That Saturday at quarter to six Miss Barlow came around carrying a green metal tray filled with small brown envelopes. They were lined up in alphabetical order, so it took a long time to get to the T's. My heart skipped a beat when she finally handed me the one with my name on it. With shaky fingers I tore off the top and withdrew my first week's wages — two five-dollar bills and two ones. A thrill ran through me at the thought that I'd get a pay packet like this every single Saturday — as long as I kept a move on.

The streetcars were crowded with tired people all glad to be going home on Saturday night. I had to stand all the way and by the time I got to my stop my arm was killing me from hanging onto the bar above my head. On my way out the middle doors I bought a whole dollar's worth of streetcar tickets from the conductor. It was the most I'd ever bought at one time, enough to last me all the next week if I didn't go anywhere but work.

Hurrying down Veeny Street, I buttoned up my sweater. A cool breeze sent coloured leaves sailing through the air. "Falling leaves . . ." I sang the popular song softly to myself, "Tumbling down . . . fading out . . . on the ground . . ."

I stepped into the kitchen just as Mum was lifting a pan of crispy bread pudding from the oven. Her face was flushed, as usual, from hurrying. I must remember, I thought worriedly, not to rush through life like Mum. For once I was glad I took after Dad. He was more of a plodder.

"Hi, Mum."

"Hello, Bea. Supper will be ready soon."

Snapping open the clasp of my worn leather purse (an inheritance from Winn) I took out a five-dollar bill and a one.

Mum was busily laying the table. I noticed the oilcloth was threadbare at the corners. "Will you cut up the bread, Bea, like a good scout?" she asked.

"Sure, Mum, but first stop for a second."

The rubber heel of her house shoe made a squeaky sound as she pivoted around to face me. I held out the six dollars. "What's this for?" she asked, without taking it.

"It's my board, Mum," I answered proudly.

"Oh, pshaw, Bea. You don't need to give me all that out of your first week's wages. Your father just got a raise to twenty dollars a week, so we're fine and dandy now."

"Well, I want to." I pressed the bills into her hand.

She stood dumbly for a minute. Then she began rolling the money between her palms in that excited way she had, as if she was making a roll-your-own cigarette. Suddenly her face lit up and her dark eyes gleamed. "I know what I'm going to do with the extra money," she said. "I'm going to put it in the bank towards a down payment on this house." She looked around the old-fashioned kitchen.

"If this place was mine," she whispered, even though we were alone in the room, "I'd make short work of that ugly tin sink and those unsightly sewer pipes from the bathroom." As if to prove her point, someone flushed the toilet and the water rushed down the pipe with a great gurgling sound. She turned away, disgusted, and glanced into the dining room. I could tell she was stripping the layers of wallpaper off in her mind's eye.

"Billy and Maude Sundy said they'd take two

hundred dollars down and the rest we could pay like rent. Then 18 Veeny Street would be ours. And, by jove, I mean to have it!"

Now she began smoothing the rolled-up bills in the palm of her hand. "You remember I was going to start a bank account when Winn was here, Bea? Well, I never did because by the time I made the payments to Eaton's Home Lover's Club for my new sewing machine there was never anything left." She paused, as if meditating. "I guess I could have done without my Singer. My mother's old treadle works as good as ever and it's a regular dust collector sitting upstairs in the hallway. Still, I get my sewing done a lot faster on the Singer. And anybody who does as much mending and sewing as I do deserves an electric machine, wouldn't you say so?"

"I sure would, Mum," I agreed.

"But now, Bea, with this extra money I can see my way clear to salt some away. I'll go straight to the bank on Monday morning and open up a house account. But we better keep it to ourselves, just in case. It'll be a secret twixt me and thee." She laughed as she used her grandmother's old-fashioned phrase.

"Yeah, Mum, twixt me and thee." I was thrilled to pieces. Imagine my board money actually helping to buy Mum her dream. I couldn't get over that.

Jumping up on the little stool that made her tall enough to reach the top of the kitchen cabinet, Mum pulled forward the metal box from the back. Lifting the lid, she carefully hid the six dollars under the rent receipts and returned the box to its place.

Stepping down, she turned to me with a strange light in her eyes. Suddenly she reached up and took my face between her work-roughened hands. "My stars, Booky," she declared in a surprised voice, "it's just this minute dawned on me. You're not a girl anymore. You're an independent woman now."

Then she threw her arms around me and gave me a tight, bone-cracking hug.

Epilogue

The war lasted six long years and one by one all the boys in our gang went off to fight for freedom. Mum's greatest fear came true when Arthur joined the navy and sailed happily away.

Suddenly the Great Depression was over. Jobs popped up like toadstools. As the boys joined the armed forces, the girls took their places at the workbench. All except Ruthie Vaughan. She joined the women's airforce and had the time of her life.

There was big money to be made in war work, but I stayed on at Eaton's and worked my way up the ladder to the grand sum of twenty-one dollars a week.

To help with the war effort, butter and sugar were rationed, so along came margarine and saccharin. You couldn't buy soap for love nor money, so detergent was invented. No more silk came from Japan, so nylon stockings were born. I'll never forget my first pair of nylons, because the thread was so strong they lasted a whole year.

At last, in 1945, the war ended and the boys came back. But not all of them. Jimmy Hobbs never returned to his mail truck. Charlie and Alvin were lost at sea. Victor Barnes came home wounded, with only one leg. And Bucky White, who was an R.A.F.

pilot, had bailed out of his flaming Spitfire and spent three years as a prisoner of war in Germany. When he came home, thin and haggard, he refused to talk about it.

My sailor brother and Georgie Dunn and Lorne Huntley, who both served in the R.C.A.F., all came back unharmed.

Lorne and I married and had two little girls. Glad married Harry Greenwood and did the same thing. Willa married Clifford Best and Wesley never got over it. Winn married an air force officer. We all quit our jobs to raise our families. That's the way it was then.

Jakey and Billy missed the war altogether because they were too young, thank goodness. They both became successful businessmen. And fathers.

Dad lived to be eighty, still insisting that World War I should have been the war to end all wars.

And Mum? What about my loving, high-strung, vivacious, black-eyed mother? Well, one day when she was hurry-hurry-hurrying, her tired heart gave up and stopped. She never did live to realize her dream of a home of her own.

Sadly, the money she had painstakingly saved in her house account went towards her funeral. And ironically, about six months after she died Dad did manage to scrape up enough money to put a down payment on 18 Veeny Street.

And I, that scatterbrain Booky? I *did* become a writer, against all odds and predictions. So, as Aunt Milly would say if only she were here, "Every cloud has a silver lining."

Bernice Thurman Hunter

When her first book was published, Bernice Thurman Hunter was astonished at the response from her readers. Now she is busy travelling to schools all over Ontario, speaking about *That Scatterbrain Booky* and its first sequel, *With Love from Booky*. Now *As Ever, Booky* rounds off the Booky story. Bernice has also written a non-Booky book, *A Place for Margaret*, with an equally appealing heroine, and is working on a sequel for that as well.